I GUESS ALL WE HAVE IS FREEDOM

"Hadazawari" ["To The Touch"] was first published in the literary magazine *Chuokoron*, 1979. "Chichi ga kieta" ["And Dad Vanished"] was first published in the literary magazine *Bungakukai*, 1980. "Jitaku no ugomeki" ["The Throes of Home"] was first published in *Chichi ga kieta*, 1981, Bungeishunju, Ltd. "Shinmetorikku" ["Symmetric"] and "Kaki no kisetsu" ["Oyster Season"] were first published in *Hadazawari*, 1980, by Chuokoronsha, Inc. All written by Katsuhiko Otsuji (a.k.a. Genpei Akasegawa).

English translation rights arranged by Kawada Shobo Shinsha Publishers through the Japan Foreign-Rights Centre.

Printed in the United States
28 27 26 25 4 3 2 1

Published by Kaya Press
www.kaya.com
Distributed by D.A.P./Distributed Art Publishers // artbook.com // (800) 388-BOOK
ISBN: 9781885030726
LCCN: 2021013995
Cover and Book Design: Hironori Oooka / oooka.jp
Cover Illustration: hagie K / hagiwarakei.com

Special thanks to Jenny Tinghui Zhang, Toshi Shibata (SCAI THE BATHHOUSE), Yui Yoshizumi, and Naoko Akasegawa.

This publication is made possible by support from the USC Dana and David Dornsife College of Arts, Letters, and Sciences; the Shinso Ito Center for Japanese Religions and Culture; the USC Department of American Studies and Ethnicity; and the USC Department of East Asian Languages and Cultures. Special thanks to the Choi Chang Soo & Yu Soon Nam Foundation and Stephen CuUnjieng for their support.

Additional funding was provided by generous contributions from: Manibha Banerjee, Lisa Chen, Judy Choi, Matthew Fargo, Sesshu Foster, Joseph Goetz, Toko Harada-Szarapka, Jean Ho, Huy Hong, Jonathan Hugo, Keesoo Huh, Mia Kang, Vandana Khanna, Seema Khurana, Swati Khurana, Seema Khurana, Nidhi Khurana,Helen Kim Lee & Stephen Lee, Sabrina Ko, Juliana Koo, Sun Hee Koo, Preity Kumar & Suzanne C. Persard, Iris Law, Helen Lee, Whakyung Lee in memory of Sonya Choi Lee, Ed Lin, Abir Majumdar, Faisal Mohyuddin, Brian Nagata, Viet Thanh Nguyen, Julia Oh, Minkyung and Yun Oh, Corey Ohama, Peter Oishi, Chez Bryan Ong, Jhani Randhawa, Prageeta Sharma,Andrew Shih, Anil Sookhoo, Patricia Wakida, Duncan Ryuken Williams, Amelia Wu & Sachin Adarkar, Anita Wu & James Spicer, Shinae Yoon, Mikoto Yoshida, Patricia & Andy Yun, and many others.

This book is published thanks to support from the Japan Foundation; the National Endowment for the Arts; the Los Angeles County Board of Supervisors through the Los Angeles County Arts Commission; the City of Los Angeles Department of Cultural Affairs; and the Community of Literary Magazines and Presses.

I GUESS ALL WE HAVE IS FREEDOM

STORIES BY

KATSUHIKO OTSUJI

Translated by Matt Fargo

KAYA PRESS

LOS ANGELES

and dad vanished

WITH A CLANG and a jolt, the outbound train leaves Mitaka Station. As we pick up speed, I start to get giddy. I know it's ridiculous for a man my age to get giddy—but that's what happens when you ride the other way.

From here in Mitaka, I've only ever taken "inbound" trains to Tokyo, but this is an "outbound" route, pointed strangely away from the city. The train clangs, and my whole worldview shifts as the familiar cityscape of Mitaka peels up from the ground and flips over like a giant page. And then the train continues flipping through page after unexpected page of a city I thought I knew. This is a special moment. When a train goes the other way, you really feel like you're moving. You get giddy.

As a boy, I loved sneaking onto horse-drawn wagons as they rolled through town. I'm pretty sure my whole conception of travel comes from this: the sensation of being conveyed through space sans the motivation of my legs. It made me giddy back then, too.

"I bet you've never even seen a horse cart," I say to Baba, my companion on today's trek.

Baba used to be a student of mine at the Art School in Tokyo. That's where I take all those "inbound" trains. Nowadays he works at a magazine. It's his day off.

"A horse cart . . . huh," he nods solemnly.

This "huh" is clearly an abbreviated version of "No, I haven't." But Baba lets the sentence trail off as if he'd never even started it. He's a tall man with beady little eyes and the telltale remnants of teenage acne on his cheeks. The magazine he edits is called *Living*. But today he's simply my boon companion.

"It's weird," I say. "It used to be totally normal to see horses walking through town, just casually dropping horseshit in the middle of the street—*plop, plop, plop*."

"That must have been wild," Baba murmurs.

"Yeah, it was wild. But think about how much wilder it would be today. There'd be horseshit everywhere. Buck-naked horseshit."

"Buck-naked?"

"Yeah. You'd be going about your day fully clothed when—*plop, plop, plop*—a bunch of horseshit would come falling out onto the street, buck-naked. If something like that happened today it would be considered criminal, unsanitary, a form of communal violence. The neighborhood association would be up in arms; the owner of the horse would be held liable . . ."

"Everyone would wind up in court!"

"Yeah! But back then nobody batted an eye. You know how people leave empty cans all over the place these days? Well imagine if all of those cans were horseshit. Raw horseshit. Uncensored, buck-naked horseshit . . ."

"You, uh . . . You probably shouldn't be saying 'horseshit' so much."

Baba is staring at the floor, embarrassed.

"Ah."

I forgot. That's a bad word. Well, nothing's wrong with the word, per se. It's the subject matter that's problematic.

"But it's still weird to me," I continue. "That whole scene—that was only thirty-odd years ago."

"Thirty-odd years, eh . . ."

Baba is twenty-five.

I don't say anything else. Instead I glance around the car, shift the overhead strap from one hand to the other. I fiddle with a button on my shirt, gaze out the window. Meanwhile the train presses onward, peeling through page after page of landscape, roiling up an exotic breeze that brushes over my cheeks. I start getting giddy again. I'm back in my childhood, smuggling myself onto horse carts . . . I'm in the second grade. Our whole class has been sent into town on poop patrol. At first we use sticks to push the horseshit into these big tin dustpans, but that gets immediately tedious, and before we know it everyone is simply scooping the stuff up with their bare hands. Human shit is repulsive because it actually looks like it's gone twisting through the body, but horseshit feels more like it went in one end and came right back out the other. There's a certain objecthood to it.

Come to think of it, in art class they used to give us this cardboard stock called "manure paper" for sketching practice. I guess all that horseshit we picked up got sent off to the horseshit factory where it was turned into manure paper. I never really thought about why they called it manure paper. Did manure paper really come from horseshit?

"Hey, you know manure paper?"

"Huh?"

"You know, that cardboard stock they used to give us in art class."

"You mean tagboard?"

"Yeah, that's right—tagboard. Tagboard . . ."

"You still thinking about horse . . . poop?"

"Nah, I was just thinking about tagboard."

I switch my grip on the overhead strap again and rub my eyes with my free hand. That's not right—I wasn't thinking about tagboard. I was thinking about wagons. About movement. About this breeze on my cheek. The wind blowing back page after page of landscape.

I remember hearing that same clang when my family moved up to Nagoya from Ōita. The trains ran on steam back then, but they still made the same clang. I remember getting to the station in the early evening, which makes this particular memory stand out. All my other memories of Ōita Station take place late at night: the absolute dead of night, just before dawn starts creeping in. Like the time my older brother graduated from middle school and moved up to Tokyo. The moon was still out, the whole town fast asleep around us. We set out for the station, our collars popped up against the cold. We didn't see a single soul until we climbed up onto the platform, where a few scattered travelers stood waiting for the train. Bare light bulbs burned in the dark. The travelers murmured in low tones, terse phrases followed by pale puffs of breath—bursts of steam from boiling kettles. At last the engine came barreling into the station like an iron lion, slowing to a hefty halt before heaving its own steamy sigh. The travelers on the platform grew tense, drawing their luggage close, animals in the presence of a great predator. Then, with one wary eye on the engine's fangs, they began gently, momentously, filing into its belly.

That's how I remember my brother's departure for Tokyo. It was the same for my sister. And likewise for my father when he got transferred. Whenever one of us left the nest, we would all wake up around four in the morning and trudge through the sleeping city to see them off. Even as a child, I could sense the gravity of these occasions. In retrospect, it's odd that the trains always came in the middle of the night. Maybe that's just how train schedules worked back then. Maybe Ōita got stuck with the short end of the timetable stick. But whatever the reason, an iron lion always came panting up in the middle of the night, a loved one would climb aboard, and then we would hurry home, our eyes on the ground as the avenue blushed with dawn.

Eventually, our whole family packed up our earthly belongings and followed my dad to Tokyo. But it was still early in the evening when we arrived at Ōita Station for that final farewell. I guess the timetables had been revised by then, making things a little easier on everyone out in Ōita. Who knows? These are all vague childhood memories, meant to be ingested with a few grains of salt.

It was the first time we'd moved in a decade. Before that, I was told, we had bounced around the belly of Japan, switching cities every couple years: from Tokyo to Yokkaichi, then Nagoya, Yokohama, Ashiya, and Moji, until at last we came to Ōita, where we spent an entire decade. I was born in Yokohama, so I didn't really remember anything until Ashiya or thereabouts.

All the family pictures from before I was born included a "maid" standing off to one side. Of course the only "maids" I'd ever encountered were characters in Victorian novels; I'd never actually seen one. On the contrary, sometimes I'd peer down the hallway and see stern, rigid faces peering through the front door, which my brother would refer to as "debt collectors." To me, however, they always just looked like the good old neighborhood grocer or the fishmonger or the owner of the local five-and-dime. Whoever it was would stand stock-still in the entryway, their face as hard and greasy as a crab shell. And as I peered back at them, the reality of poverty and all its attendant complexes would accost me with such intensity that I had to bury my feelings deep down, to keep them safe.

"Keeping your complexes safe" is a weird way to describe it, but my complexes helped sustain me. It was, of course, a negative sort of sustenance, and I suffered from a serious bedwetting problem up until the year we moved. It happened every single night all the way through middle school—sometimes even two or three times in the same night. The stench of ammonia followed me around everywhere. Our family slept in three rooms, and the tatami mat in the room where I slept soon began to buckle from all the liquid. When one spot became too warped, I would move to another. After ten years of this, the entire floor was deformed by my urine. It's incredible to think about now. All these years later, I'm still kind of frightened by my own body. But back then I managed to strike a balance between the excesses of my monstrous body and the pressures of poverty. It was a perilous tightrope to walk.

When my family finally moved out of Ōita, ten years' worth of acquaintances showed up at the station to see us off. I had a lot of siblings, each with their own cadre of friends, so the sendoff looked more like a parade. I was the fifth oldest—there was also a sixth and a seventh—and I had my own big gang of buddies. Buddies from whom I kept my complexes hidden. My best friend, my second-best friend, the friend who was actually my favorite, the one who was actually my second-favorite—they had all gathered en masse to say goodbye. It was a rowdy scene, and I didn't feel sad or nostalgic in the least. It almost felt like we were all about to go on a trip together. Of course that wasn't the case: I was moving to a faraway town and wouldn't see any of them again. But it wasn't until that clang, right as the train jolted into motion, that I realized what was happening.

Ah! It hit me.

I was standing on the deck between train cars, at the same level as the station platform. The platform began scrolling sideways, my friends' faces panning past me one after another until they were a little group in the distance.

Ah! I thought again. *Hold on. This isn't how it's supposed to end. There are probably a million things I forgot to do.*

The shock of this realization caused me to reach out with one hand, but there was nothing for me to grab, so I ended up standing there with my hand awkwardly extended. Everyone at the station started waving back. The steel wheels turned and rumbled beneath me as the entire scene slipped off into the distance. My tranquil expression fell away. The notion that I might have made an irrevocable mistake washed over me in a cold sweat. But the train continued clanging inexorably down the rails, my hand still reaching and flapping about in the wind. The station contracted into a tiny spot in the distance until all that remained was the empty landscape sliding by outside. I felt like I had accidentally boarded some precarious spaceship. And that's how we made our way from Ōita to Nagoya.

⊙⊙⊙

At least that's how I remember it: standing on a train at Ōita Station, the giant steel wheels suddenly clanging into motion.

The wheels on this train from Mitaka are gently shaking the landscape outside the window.

"Man, going the other way can be fun," I say to Baba. "I guess travel isn't always about going in the direction you want."

"Huh?"

I've caught Baba off guard. But nothing follows his "huh." It's just a question mark. Come to think of it, I haven't been relating any of my thoughts to him—about Ōita Station, or steam engines, or the rumbling of these wheels. So I clarify:

"I just mean that travel is basically about moving."

"Moving . . . ?"

"Not just moving, but moving the other way. All you have to do is move the other way and voila—you're traveling."

"Oh no," Baba balks. "Is this some kind of lesson?"

"Not a lesson, really. Although I guess it could be edifying . . ."

"Moving the other way, huh?"

"Yeah, moving the other way. Moving the other way means you're traveling; you're on a trip. For example, um . . . imagine you're at home. And you have to go to the bathroom. But instead of taking the direct path down the hallway, you climb up into the attic and then back down into the bathroom through a hatch."

"Man, you're always so . . . radical."

"It's a bit radical, I guess. Call it conceptual travel."

"Ah—we're talking about art."

"Yeah, art. If you did it right."

"So if you broke into your own bedroom through the window, would that turn your bed into a sleeping car?"

"A sleeping car! I like it."

"Like on the Orient Express."

"Ha ha, your own homemade Orient Express."

⊙⊙⊙

Baba and I are riding the other way today in order to scope out a municipal graveyard named Hachiōji Cemetery. This past spring, at age eighty, my dad drew his last breath and moved on to the next life. He slipped out through some gap in his body, never to return. Dad was a skinny man, his flesh stretched tight around his bones. For the last year of life he couldn't even get out of bed, his body pulling so thin and taut around him that he must have had a hard time finding a gap out of which to slip. At least that's how it seemed to me, after he died, when the eyelids we'd meticulously shut began to dry and pull back open, the whites of his eyes peering out between.

He died at night. I was drinking shōchū when it happened.

Earlier that evening, my mom had phoned to tell me that the end was near. In hushed tones, she informed me that the neighborhood doctor had arrived. Dad had lost consciousness, and things were not looking good.

As I was hanging up the phone, I realized that the normal thing to do here was to drop everything and race frantically to Yokohama. But I'd pretty much resigned myself to his death by then, and had a hard time feeling frantic. I imagined myself frantically arriving on the scene, and in my head this franticness seemed so overwrought that I was embarrassed just imagining it.

Dad had been dying for a while. For the last few years, or maybe even longer—from all the way back when the war ended and he lost his job in the chaos that followed—a couple millimeters of him had been dying every day. The last time I'd seen him was in January, some thirty years after the end of the war. It was my first visit in a while, and my immediate reaction when I saw him was: *Oh man, he's been doing a lot of dying.* He had simply stared back at me as if to say, "I'm getting pretty dead these days."

All of this came back to me as I hung up the phone with my mom. Then I went out to drink shōchū with my friend, as originally planned. Not saké. Potato shōchū.

Dad was from Kagoshima, the heart of shōchū country, and apparently men from Kagoshima are born with a certain restlessness. His older brother sailed to America, and his kid brother emigrated to Manchuria. My dad himself never left Japan, but he did drift up to Tokyo. I'm pretty sure it was that same wanderlust at work.

He must have been in his late teens at the time. He found work doing odd jobs for a family of nouveau riche, who had just moved to the city themselves. According to the stories he used to tell, Dad worked so hard polishing their fancy lamps that his entire body would be sore at the end of the day. All this hard work must have made an impression on his employers, because they eventually offered to pay his way through college.

One day, Dad and I were walking through Kanda when he pointed at a building and said:

"That's where I used to go to school!"

The building he'd pointed at was Meiji University. But then the nouveau riche family went bankrupt and Dad found himself pushing their oxcart as they skipped town under the cover of night, his dream of higher education receding into the distance with every step. Back then, I was neither flesh nor bone; I was but an invisible speck, floating around in the air above that oxcart.

After drinking my fill of shōchū, I set out for my brother's apartment in Yokohama. It was late in the evening by the time I arrived, and Dad had already drawn his last breath.

My brother was away on a business trip when it happened; his wife and daughter were in their respective bedrooms. Mom had been feeding Dad porridge, but he was having a hard time getting it down, so she'd gone to the kitchen to reheat it. By the time she got back, he was gone.

She related all of this to me in a whisper. A white handkerchief lay over his face. It looked like a heaping bowl of rice. We were all aware that he was dead, but for some reason everyone spoke in hushed tones. Whenever one of us got up to go to the kitchen or the restroom, the sound would reverberate throughout the apartment. Instead of something having just ended, it felt like something was about to begin.

On our way home from the funeral, we stopped by the Yokohama docks, still dressed in mourning attire. On the pier was a small park, and the people there stared as we huddled together in a little black brood. Industrial cranes and warehouses loomed in the distance. We had brought along a photo of Dad. Something about his somber portrait seemed at odds with the ripe sea breeze. It felt out of place, as if the wind was causing the photographic paper to undergo some secondary chemical process. This sense of being out of place—to me, it seemed to summarize all of my dad's misfortunes.

He'd worked here on the docks. And while "working on the docks" might conjure up the image of a tan, broad-shouldered longshoreman with a handkerchief tied around his brow, Dad was merely a paper pusher at one of the port's warehouses. His career took him from Tokyo to Yokkaichi, then Nagoya, Yokohama, Ashiya, and Moji, before landing at last in Ōita. After the war, every subsequent move he made ended up being a mistake. Poverty beat him down, his posture slowly bowing until he curled up and withered away. I guess he wasn't really prepared to deal with the chaos that came in the wake of a war. He might have led a perfectly happy life, if it weren't for all that upheaval. But that's not the way the world works.

"Hey, look—an ad for a cemetery."

This time Baba is trying to strike up conversation. A poster is dangling down from the center of the aisle, right next to his strap.

"Oh. Hey."

I reach out and grab a corner of the poster.

A dialogue with nature. Peace in the park.

TOKOROZAWA FUNERARY GARDEN
Currently taking reservations for 700 plots

I release the poster and it goes back to wiggling in the breeze.

"I only recently started noticing these," I say.

"Do they make you want to buy one?"

"Buy one? We're not talking cameras here."

"Cameras?"

"Yeah, a camera is something I actually want. I openly ogle camera advertisements. But who's going to go around ogling cemetery ads."

"Insane . . ."

"Insane?"

"Ogling cemetery advertisements," Baba clarifies, "sounds pretty insane."

"I don't know about 'insane.'"

"Well, it would at least be weird."

"I guess," I concede. "Anyway—there sure are a lot of cemeteries out there. Once you're in the market for a grave, you start seeing advertisements for them everywhere."

It's true: these days I walk about in a state of sustained disbelief regarding the sheer number of advertisements for cemeteries out there. I don't think I'd ever noticed a single one before.

I had this same experience with pawnshops, years ago. This was in my early twenties, at that age when you're done with college but still living like a college kid, so you don't have a lot of cash, and from time to time you run out of things to eat, your sense of hunger growing in inverse proportion to the amount of food in your pantry. Hunger is the kind of thing that swells up inside you as an absence. And so I found myself being sucked into the negative space of that vendor of absence: the pawnshop.

I took the only suit left in my dresser that retained any sort of crease, folded it more neatly than I had ever folded it before, and ventured out to hock it, making my way through city streets I had hitherto wandered completely oblivious to the abundance of pawnshop ads that now seemed to pop up on every fence and telephone pole.

And that's what it's been like with cemetery ads.

"Hey, Baba," I say. "Which do you think has more advertisements: cemeteries or condominiums?"

"Huh?"

"I've been seeing a lot of both these days—to the point where they sort of bleed together, in my mind."

"Ah, gotcha."

"Am I right?"

"Yeah, I guess they do have a similar feel. Same for wedding venues."

"Oh yeah, those bridal reception halls! What is it about them . . . ?"

"I think they just look the same. They must all use the same color scheme or something."

"The color scheme, yeah. There's also something about the way they're printed . . ."

"It's the finish. They all have a similar gleam."

"Yeah, that gleam. The shimmer is the same. All three kinds of posters use that same technique—it's weird."

"I wonder how come?"

"I don't know. I mean, all advertisements go out of their way to sparkle at you. But there's something distinct about the sparkle of those three genres."

"A similar ritziness."

"Exactly. I guess ritziness is a measurable effect. As is expensiveness."

"Expensiveness, yeah."

"Cemetery plots are like condos: the sunny south-facing ones cost more."

"Seriously?"

"Yeah. As if they were made for real people."

"Man. You think the city graveyard will be like that?"

"Nah, public graves aren't condos—they're more like housing projects. They hold a lottery for plots."

The cemetery ad is flapping around in the middle of the aisle. Further down the car, an advertisement for condos flutters, too. Also wiggling in the breeze: an ad for some sort of bridal reception venue. The train cuts onward, my mouth engaged in its own flapping as I jaw off about cemeteries. But while my mouth continues about its business, my eyes are stopping at each station we pass, my mind pausing with it in a slideshow of station names:

Musashi-Sakai. Back when I was in art school, a buddy of mine used to live here. He was a dumpy little guy, all hunched over and bug-eyed as if he'd just escaped from Notre Dame de Paris. And he was obsessed with coffee. One Christmas evening, to impress a girl, he drank twenty-one cups in a single sitting.

Higashi-Koganei. I've never seen this station before. It used to be that Musashi-Koganei followed Musashi-Sakai. I remember the interval between these stations was extremely long, punctuated only by the steel tower of a power substation, looming in the distance like a mirage.

Musashi-Koganei. I'll never forget this station. It's where I lived when I first moved to the city. I shared a tiny studio apartment with a friend for thirty bucks a month. We were both enrolled at the Musashino School of Art. The school has since moved to a huge complex at Takanodai, but back then it was just a rickety one-story building ten minutes north of Kichijōji Station. Rumor had it that before the war it had been an army barrack or a boarding school for girls, and the hallway running through it felt like a country lane: long and winding and riddled with puddles. All the windows were cracked and covered with graffiti. There was so much paint on them that they looked like stained glass.

Pretty much everybody who applied to the school got accepted. I remember the entrance exam involved sculpting a classic plaster bust. For the written portion, we were given a piece of cheap newsprint and told to write an essay. I think the topic was "On Art" or something innocuous like that. Halfway through the test, a bunch of kids from the neighborhood burst into the room. The proctor, who had been sitting next to the lectern reading his newspaper, started hollering at them:

"For Chrissakes, kids! Get outta here! We're in the middle of something important!"

The kids had yelled right back:

"But so-and-so said so-and-so did such-and-such to so-and-so!"

I don't remember exactly what they said—I was in the middle of an "important" exam, after all—but the kids eventually went clattering back out on their little wooden sandals. Then they snuck back in for another peek, squealed when they got caught, and clattered away again.

I genuinely liked that school, but quickly recognized the absurdity of learning art in a classroom setting. I was also running out of money. After that first year, I dropped out.

It was my dad who had scraped together the funds for me to go to college in the first place. I remember the gesture took me completely by surprise. In that small stack of bills he handed me, I could feel the heat of some nameless passion. My older brother was the one who should have pursued an education, but when he came of age we were still in the depths of poverty, so he had to forfeit any academic ambitions. It was those same depths of poverty that brought my family together in the middle of the night to see him off to Tokyo. I suspect that if my older brother had been the one to go to college, he would have made our dad proud.

By the time I came of age, my family's poverty had lost the modifier of "depths." And I wanted to go to "art school" of all places. Art school is still kind of a punch line, but back then it was considered laughably pointless. Even if you managed to graduate, all you'd have to show for your trouble would be vague career goals and zero chance of economic advancement. But I'd been praised for my drawing ability since I was a kid, and by the time I'd grown into a pasty, shy, bedwetting young man, art seemed like it might be my only shot in life. And so my impoverished dad somehow scraped together the unrealistic sum of money needed to send me to the art school of my choice. I was overjoyed, of course, but at the same time I felt a little unsettled by the whole thing. Thanks to my dad's contribution, together with my own meager savings, I was able to matriculate. In retrospect, that little stack of tuition money contained all his hopes and dreams. Not his pride or anything like that—more like his vague, unrealized aspirations. He'd been into haiku since he was a kid.

⊙⊙⊙

The train pulls out of Musashi-Koganei Station.

"Ever heard of Koganei Kojirō?" I ask Baba out of the blue.

"Who's that?"

"I don't actually know much about him, but I used to live here in Koganei. I was at their big summer festival once, and these two yakuza-looking guys started getting into it. I remember one of them was all up in the other's face, yelling about: 'Well I'm related to Koganei Kojirō!' I didn't know who that was at the time, but later I found out that Koganei Kojirō was an old-school yakuza boss."

"I've never heard of him."

Well that little anecdote bombed. Why was I blabbing on about Koganei Kojirō—I hadn't thought about him in years. The memory just bubbled up and spilled straight out of my mouth.

Baba stands there in silence. He's staring out the window, his lanky figure hunched over a subway strap, free hand stuffed in a pocket. I wonder if he's deep in thought about Koganei Kojirō. I bet I've given him a tiny complex about his ignorance of Koganei Kojirō, and now he's squeezing that complex with the hand in his pocket. I've done a bad thing.

"Hey," I say.

"Huh?"

"Um . . . Koganei! It sure has changed."

This time I've blurted out something tremendously pedestrian. I was trying to contextualize the whole yakuza anecdote, but I got nervous the moment I opened my mouth. I feel like a baseball player who popped up a fly ball on their first at-bat and then committed an error trying to field a ground ball because they were still feeling self-conscious about their showing at the plate. So I take a minute to gather myself. I watch the scenery scroll by, pretending to notice all the things that have changed about Koganei. It doesn't help, though. I'm still nervous.

Then again, maybe this is just what travel feels like. Maybe this is the sensation of moving in an unexpected direction.

"It's weird," I say, "the different things your mind can mull over all at once."

This time I'm not fooling around. I've gotten out in front of the grounder, fielded it with both hands, and turned to throw it toward first base. Except I must have thrown the ball too hard, because Baba looks confused:

"Huh?"

"I just mean that our brains are constantly off thinking about all these totally unrelated subjects. Unprovoked. Without pause. Or maybe our brains pause from time to time and we just don't remember."

"Uh . . . okay?"

"Like, you know how when you forget something, you can never actually remember the moment you forgot it?"

"Well, yeah. If you could remember when you forgot things, you'd never forget anything."

"Exactly. Which is why we're constantly forgetting stuff."

"It's the same as not remembering the moment you fall asleep."

"Precisely. If you were aware of that moment, you'd never actually fall asleep. Have you ever fainted before, Baba?"

"Nope."

"Well I did once. On purpose. I was always a little anemic as a kid, and if I stood up and stretched too quickly I'd get light-headed. Usually I'd just sit back down again until the dizziness went away, but one day I got curious about what would happen if I didn't sit down—you know how kids are. Anyway, one moment I was standing there stretching, and the next moment I went blank."

"What happened?"

"I'd been standing next to the fireplace. It was still autumn, so the fire wasn't lit or anything, but when I came to I had my face in the ashes. I had no idea how I'd gotten there. I guess I just fell flat on my face. A cloud of ash was still floating all around me."

"Kinda scary."

"Yeah, it was—but only when I thought about it later. I never tried anything like that again."

The train is almost at Kokubunji. After Kokubunji comes Kunitachi, Tachikawa, Hino, and Toyoda. After that: Hachiōji.

⦿⦿⦿

Dad had his first fall two months before he passed. This was when my parents were still in Nagoya. And it wasn't really a "fall" because he hadn't been standing; he'd been sitting with my mom, eating his lunch. Mom got up to get some soy sauce from the kitchen, and by the time she got back, his forehead was flat on the table.

He was alone when he died, too. Nobody saw it happen. It was the same with his first "fall." It took a while for my mom to even realize what had happened, when she finally returned from the kitchen.

"Honey?" she'd asked. "Are you asleep?"

He hadn't answered.

Later, the doctor told us that his fall was due to a softening of the brain. Dad came around relatively fast, but he was bedridden from that point onward. He'd hurt his hip a few years prior and was already spending a lot of time in bed. By then it was just him and my mom living alone in the Nagoya projects.

When we first moved up to Nagoya from Ōita, we were still one big family. My older brother remained in Tokyo, but a gimpy uncle had appeared in his stead. At times there would be nine people sharing our little two-bedroom apartment in the public housing projects behind the Nagoya docks. Everyone headed out during the day, but at night there would be nine sleeping bodies packing the gaps between furniture, the apartment accruing the mass of a black hole from which no light could escape.

The Yokohama projects served as a sort of finishing school, where timid kids were molded into independent adults. One by one, we each left the apartment to make our fortunes. I moved to Tokyo in the thrall of that rickety old art school; one of my sisters worked the till at a pachinko parlor and put herself through college in Nagoya; all the other sisters got married off, vanishing from the apartment one after another. Then Typhoon Vera came and destroyed the neighborhood. My parents were lucky enough to find housing in another project further inland, but by then all their kids had decamped save for my youngest brother, who had just finished middle school. Eventually even he headed to Tokyo to make a life for himself. And thus, like a star gone into nova—its exterior layers blown out into the void, leaving only the white dwarf at its core—all that remained in that Nagoya apartment was our parental nucleus.

When Dad's forehead hit the table that first time, it was like he was pressing an emergency call button. Seven tiny wires reached out from that table to seven red lamps around the country, each of which began blinking in a state of emergency. All seven of his kids, managing their own respective lives in different corners of Japan, suddenly found themselves conferring amongst this flickering red light. Conversations flew back and forth between those of us in Tokyo and those of us in Yokohama, those of us in Saitama and those of us in Nagoya.

Eventually mom gave us the doctor's prognosis: the worst had passed and Dad was stable for the time being, but it was unlikely he would ever recover. If we were hoping to relocate him, we would have to do so as soon as possible; he might not be able to handle a big move further down the line. And even an immediate relocation ran the risk of some unforeseen calamity.

The phrase "unforeseen calamity" sounded like it was set in gothic type. The ink was spread on the form, ready to be pressed onto paper. We stared directly at this ominous font and decided to move my dad anyway. The plan was to transfer him to the Yokohama housing complex where my oldest brother had an apartment. All of us kids either lived in public housing or rented. We figured that if we had to move Dad somewhere cramped, the least we could do was take him to the home of his favorite son.

That same day we all gathered in my parents' Nagoya apartment while our white dwarf continued its steady spin. It was the first time in ten years we had all been together, and with the entire family crammed into one room, there was literally nowhere to move. It was as if the old black hole had formed again, ten years' worth of time compacted so tightly that the little living room began to shine. In the glow of this compressed light, we couldn't figure out whether to be happy or sad. And so we sat there wearing the austere expressions of sages atop a mountain.

From his bed in the next room, Dad gazed at each of our faces one by one. He seemed to be able to tell us apart, but he didn't say a word. Mom told us he was usually more talkative. She said he was having trouble expressing himself at the moment, and that he was just happy to see us. The way he stared, though, you could tell he was no longer scrutinizing, ruminating, or engaging with anything. He was just looking. Everything he saw seemed to surprise him. From his bed, he gazed up at each of us children as though we were gods. His expression made us feel divine. I went to his bedside and tried speaking to him, but it immediately felt absurd. He could hear each individual utterance, but to him my words must have sounded like the proclamations of a deity. "Oh yes, it's the god of bedwetting," his face seemed to say, staring up at me from his pillow. In my dad's trembling eyes, I could see the reflection of the divine light I emanated.

One of my brothers went and borrowed a van from work. We folded down the rear seat and made a bed in the back with a couple of futon mattresses. Then my older brother and I carried our dad down from the second floor. We grabbed the ends of his futon and lifted it up like a stretcher, but it was soft and bendy and almost impossible to carry. The whole thing sank in the middle, causing my dad to fold at the hips. We frantically tried to get underneath him, only to have the futon bend back the other way. It felt like we were trying to carry a giant drop of water, the delicate surface tension of which might break at any moment.

After we'd hoisted the water drop into the rear of the van, my mom got into the passenger seat next to my brother. I lay down in the back with the water drop. The water drop gazed up at the apartment building, transfixed.

I was worried about getting carsick. My stomach was already on edge from the strange sensation of lying on soft futons in the back of a van with my pants riding up on me. From where I lay, I could see the roofline of the apartment complex as well as the clouds above. I was almost certain I would be sick once we started moving.

My sisters were waving at us. Dad waved back with his fingers. The futons shuddered beneath me as the van began to move, the roofline shaking and sliding to the side. *I'm going to be sick,* I thought again, but I was still all right. The clouds dangled down from the sky, making me even more anxious. I'd spent all three years of high school in Nagoya, and for several years after moving to Tokyo I'd returned for the summer and winter holidays. But now the familiar cityscape was only partially visible through the bottom of the window, its topmost crest squiggling along beneath a cloud-filled sky. I anxiously eyed that top ten percent of the city, trying to remember what the other ninety percent looked like. I'd been down some of these streets a hundred times, while others I'd only heard of. The names of districts and thoroughfares flitted by on telephone poles. This partial panorama was reflected in the water drop beside me, refracting and reversing, spinning as it shone. Then, all at once, the city went stuttering out of the frame and we were left with an empty sky.

The van stopped shaking once we hit the smooth tarmac of the freeway and stayed that way until we pulled over at a rest stop in Fujikawa. We were about halfway to our destination. Stretched out in the back of the van, I let out a sigh of relief. If we were already at the rest area, I probably wasn't going be carsick after all. We had avoided the "unforeseen calamity." The letterpress was not in motion—at least not yet.

My younger brother took a deep breath and opened his door. My older brother stepped out, followed by mom. Finally the rear door popped open, and all at once I could see one hundred percent of the world again. I shimmied out feet-first and turned my nauseous body right-side up. The clouds rotated back to their proper position, and I inhaled my own deep breath. But Dad could still only see the top ten percent of the world. He lay there on his futons, gazing through the window at that uneasy fraction.

Once out of the van, I could see Mount Fuji looming before us. It was so massive that for a while I just stood there, stunned.

Back before television or color photography, Mount Fuji was considered an A-list celebrity. Even teenagers would get all starstruck around it. In middle school, when we were living in Ōita, one of my friends took a trip to Tokyo with his dad, and when he got back, the first thing everyone asked him was:

"Did you see Mount Fuji?"

I remember my friend had just nodded slowly, spreading his arms as wide as they could go as he described how huge the mountain had looked from the train. We all listened to his tale enthralled, our eyes tracing the shapes his arms made in the air.

And now this celebrity was right in front of me. I could see every detail—it was like looking at the mountain through the viewfinder of a camera. Mount Fuji in the flesh. The weather was perfect; the mountain was massive. It wasn't merely massive—it was imposing. For a while all we could do was stand there, agog. The oldest brother, the bedwetter, the guy driving the station wagon: three brothers lost in a mountain's grandeur. Our own respective heights were the exact inverse of our ages, a clear manifestation of Japan's nutritional situation in the years following the war. Three brothers gawking at Fuji's hugeness, grateful for the alpine air. We were all glad to have made it this far without incident, and so we sat down on the grass, side by side, stretching out our legs and munching on the rice balls mom had prepared that morning.

Mom sat in the back of the car next to Dad. Peeling open her own rice ball, she said:

"Look, honey! It's Mount Fuji. What a gorgeous view."

The crisp air carried her voice right to us. We thought we heard our dad mumble some sort of reply, but it might have just been a trick of the mind—a voice assembled from our memories of his accent and diction:

"Mm-hmm."

His three sons sat in the grass, munching rice balls and gazing back at their father.

My brother's apartment was a fifth-floor walkup in a five-story building. The stairs changed direction at each landing, so to get to the fifth floor, you had to navigate a total of eight switchbacks. This time my younger brother and I took charge of the futon stretcher while my older brother ran up the stairs ahead of us. As we heaved that flaccid water drop up step by step, I was reminded of a part-time job I once had, hauling lumber at a department store. After the store closed for the night, we had to carry these long two-by-fours up to the roof. The wood itself wasn't all that heavy; the hard part was getting up the stairs without scuffing up the walls. The switchbacks were the crux. You could zoom straight up the flights of stairs, but when you got to a landing you had to slow down, meticulously turning through that narrow space. As the ends of the beams swung within inches of the white walls, you had to lower your center of gravity and solidify your stance like a bird coming in for a landing. The stairs were all flights and landings. And so the word "landing" was forever imprinted on my body, stamped by the lumber that dug into my shoulder. On that job, the walls had been more important than the wood, but this time our "lumber" was more important than the walls. It didn't matter if we scuffed up the paint so long as we didn't damage our cargo.

You could still see Mount Fuji from my brother's fifth floor flat, although it was much further off. You had to stand up to catch a glimpse of it; otherwise the balcony would block your view.

We installed Dad in the tatami room, and thus he was filled with joy. He never got to his feet again; he simply lay quietly on the tatami mats in what was to him the most lavish place on earth.

The color returned to his face. Two weeks later, he celebrated his eightieth birthday. Then, in the spring, still filled with joy, he lost consciousness.

◎◎◎

At last the train rolls into Hachiōji Station. Baba hasn't said anything for a while now. He's always been the silent type. Come to think of it, I haven't said anything for a while either. At some point I turned into a silent type, too. We get off the train and ask a cop for directions to the cemetery. He informs us that even though the exit we're at is called "Hachiōji Cemetery," we should have stayed on the train for two more stops and debarked at Takao Station, which is next to the actual cemetery. Which makes no sense whatsoever, but here we are: we've already exited the ticket gate and are feeling a bit peckish—why not tuck into a little sushi?

I get a red tuna bowl. Baba orders the deluxe chirashi.

"Wow, the deluxe, eh?" I ask.

"Huh? "

"You sure about that order?"

Historically, I've always been wary of sushi prices.

"It's fine," Baba says, coolly perusing the menu. "Look—this place actually has another level above deluxe."

I take a closer look at the menu and sure enough, the "deluxe" is even cheaper than the normal option. I feel disoriented, take a sip of tea.

"So I hear you're getting married next month?"

"Yep," Baba says. "Sure am . . ."

"And your wife's from Chiba?"

"Yeah. From Matsudo."

"When's the wedding?"

"I don't think we're gonna have one."

"Oh, really?"

"It's just such a hassle . . ."

"Sure, nobody's ever dying to go through the ordeal of a wedding. It's something you do for your parents, right?"

"All I have is my mom, and she seems indifferent."

"Well, what about the bride's parents?"

"Same there."

"Seriously?"

"Yeah, they don't care."

"You did meet them, though? When you went to Chiba?"

"Yeah, we went and did all our introductions."

"I thought country folk were strict about their betrothals and nuptials and all that."

"Not really. I mean, they're cool with us not having a wedding, so . . ."

"I can't believe they'd be okay with that. What did you say? Did you actually tell them, 'We're not having a wedding?'"

"We didn't come right out and say it or anything. We just kind of chatted and drank some saké together."

"And her father never asked you about wedding plans?"

"Nah. He actually seemed kind of shy about the whole thing. He asked that I treat his daughter well and that was that."

"Huh. So it's not a problem if you don't have a wedding . . . ?"

"Man, are you really that into weddings? I'm starting to get the sense that you want us to have a ceremony just for you."

"No, no, I just always thought that weddings were this huge ordeal because of parents and all their expectations. Especially with country folk."

"Not really."

"Hmm."

My tuna bowl arrives. I love red tuna bowls. I love them precisely because they feature the red part of the tuna. I feel like a whole bowl of the fancy white toro would actually be a bit of a turnoff. But I'm still hung up on Baba's wedding. I thought fathers were supposed to be all demanding and unyielding. Maybe the world has changed . . . "What about your dad, Baba? Oh wait, you said you didn't . . ."

"Yeah, I grew up with a single mom."

"Sorry, sorry."

"No worries."

"It's just that in movies or whatever, whenever a father has to give away his daughter, he usually gets all contrary and obstinate and ends up making these wild demands. At least that's my idea of how a father is supposed to act . . ."

"Yeah, but that's just the movies."

"Sure, it's just the movies, but . . . Yeah, I guess you're right.

That's just how dads are in movies."

"People aren't really like that anymore."

"Aren't they, though?"

"I mean, I didn't have a dad, so I can't say for sure, but . . ."

"Right . . ."

"But *you* had one, right?" Baba asks. "I mean—sorry, that sounded a little insensitive . . ."

"No, don't worry."

"What was it like?"

"Well, yeah, it's true—I did have a dad. But it was almost like he wasn't there."

"Why's that?"

"Well, a dad represents money. An estate. So when there's no money or estate to speak of, the dad doesn't really have a voice."

"Ah . . ."

"I mean, he might say things, but his opinions don't hold much weight."

"I guess there's a certain freedom in that."

"Yeah, that's right. Freedom. I guess all we have is freedom."

"Nothing but freedom."

"Kind of sad, right? Having nothing but freedom? No money, no possessions, no power—just plain old freedom."

I pause for a sip of tea. It's bitter. The green powder has settled to the bottom of my deep ceramic cup. I take another sip. Baba also pauses for a couple sips of his own.

"So why are dads something you're supposed to be scared of?"

I ask.

"Got me."

"I don't get it. The dads in movies and on TV are always these intimidating figures you're supposed to be rebelling against. I'm just not convinced that dads like that really exist."

"Oh, they exist. In the movies, at least."

"Now you're being sarcastic."

"I'm not being sarcastic. I never had a father of my own, so whenever I'd see one on TV, I'd think, 'Oh, I guess that's what a dad is supposed to be like . . . ' I had to use my imagination."

"Yeah, same here. I mean, I had the real deal, but I still had to use my imagination."

"The real deal?"

"Well, 'the real deal' is kind of a weird way to put it, but still . . . He was the real McCoy, you know? My dad was the genuine article. I feel like most dads out there still harbor some illusion about how a father figure is supposed to act."

"This is starting to sound academic."

"I'm serious—the power of money and property has a natural manifestation, and that manifestation is this archetype of the demanding patriarch."

"A natural manifestation . . ."

"Yeah. A patriarch can't be careless with his money and property. He's gotta be arrogant, didactic, shout at people. It's all part of the effort to replicate himself."

"Ah—the reproductive urge."

"Yeah, something like that. And the natural manifestation of that urge is this archetype of a 'Father.' But when there's no inheritance to speak of, there's no point in shouting at anyone."

"But on TV, even the dads with no money like to shout."

"True, true . . . But the shouting rings kind of hollow when there's no capital behind it."

"Ha—I like the idea that money is a prerequisite for shouting."

"Yeah, I guess it's kind of funny. But it does explain why a lot of dads feel the need to build up their own patriarchal facades."

"Like bronze busts."

"Yeah, exactly. It's a completely hollow effigy, but in order to properly bronze it, they have to boss their families around."

"And your dad never built a bronze bust for himself?"

"Nope—all we had was the real deal. My dad wasn't about to go bronzing any busts. Every once in a while he'd remember that he was supposed to be building an effigy, and he'd try to have opinions or enforce rules. But there was never any money behind it, so nothing got bronzed."

"That's amazing."

"Even if I'd wanted some bust to admire, I knew I was barking up the wrong tree. All I had to work with was the real deal."

"You think dads these days are still bronzing busts?"

"I don't know. Where would you even keep a big old bust in this day and age?"

"Your kids wouldn't be able to keep their hands off it."

"Ha ha—they'd go straight for it."

"And the thing about bronze busts is that once you've touched one, you realize that that's all they are. Bronze."

"A bronze bust, once touched . . ."

At this point I've finished my tuna bowl. I put down my chopsticks and sip my bitter, sunken tea in silence. Baba still has about a third of his deluxe chirashi left.

"Want some?" he asks.

"No thanks. Hurry up and eat, though."

I stare at a white piece of squid in his bowl. A white piece of squid on a white bed of rice. Resting there, it looks like a white handkerchief over a face . . .

We use the north exit at Takao Station. From the moment we step out of the turnstile, something feels different about the place. The pillars holding up the roof of the station are made of wood, their dark brown patina betraying the age of the building. I feel as though I've been whisked back to my childhood. I take a few more steps and turn around to admire the station from afar: a rare specimin of wooden Japanese architecture in a train station. It almost looks like a Shinto shrine. *Nice job, Takao,* I think to myself.

Takao is pretty far out in the boonies. I've only ever heard its name in announcements for "Takao-bound" trains, but now that we've ridden all the way out here to the end of the line, I'm glad we made the trip. It's like meeting a celebrity in real life. I almost feel shy.

We ask another cop how to get to Hachiōji Cemetery, and he explains that we need to get on the bus for Zōkei University.

"Alternately," he amends, "it's about a forty-minute walk."

We decide to hoof it. Honestly, I love towns like this, where the mountains seem to roll right up to the city limits. Being surrounded by mountains might sound claustrophobic, but it's actually quite liberating. Downtown Tokyo, where there's nary a mountain to be seen, feels much more oppressive.

We leave the station and start up a gentle slope, our breath turning white in the mid-October air. I imagine how pretty the Zōkei University campus must be. Even though we're still technically in Tokyo, the air is brisk and clean. It's mountain air. This little slope we're ascending probably forms a foothill to some mountain.

I like hills. I like going up them, and I like coming back down. Just walking up a hill gives me a thrill. I feel the same way about second floors. There's something secretive about them. Single-story homes are plagued with ennui; all the excitement is up on the second floor. My heart jumps every time I see a staircase. I'm a sucker for a good multi-level building, but what really gets me are multi-level towns. There's no joy in a flat town. A flat town feels like it's filled with nothing but work. Hilly towns, on the other hand, brim with adventure.

Before my family moved to Ōita, we lived in a hill-filled town called Moji. Our house stood on an incline, and all the streets around us were sloped. This made Moji feel like a two- or three-story house. I was still young back then—this was before kindergarten—so I never really got to experience any of the city's flatter districts. Instead, I spent all my time exploring the nearby neighborhoods, venturing down one sloping road then back up another. Never have I enjoyed living anywhere so much as Moji.

A few years ago I had to go to Shimoseki for work. Shimoseki is right next to Moji, even though Moji is on the island of Kyūshū and Shimoseki is on the island of Honshū. The two towns straddle either side of the Kanmon Strait. It was my first time in Shimoseki, and I couldn't believe how much it looked like Moji. Once you get a little inland, hills start popping up everywhere. Walking around, I got lost in a tangle of inclines, and for a moment it felt like I was back in the Moji of my childhood, wandering among its playful, dizzying slopes.

The streets here in Takao aren't dizzying at all; they just rise lazily into the hills. Somewhere up this hill, a new cemetery is under construction, though the phrase "new cemetery construction" has a weird ring to it.

As the restless rumble of traffic slowly slips into the distance, storefronts and billboards for gravestones begin to appear one after another. All of them feature modern-looking designs. I didn't expect so many of them, and begin to speculate about the scale of the cemetery—the sheer infrastructure of dead people required to support all these businesses.

We are almost there.

◉◉◉

If a grave were a part of a house, it would be the bath. This occurred to me while I was scrubbing my tub. In a house, the bath is the only place you can just leave your clothes behind and exist, completely naked. In a city, that space is the grave: a room entombing your bare body in tile, hard and slick and white as your bones. It's a waterproof space, encased in stone. A bath is a grave—this occurred to me while I was scrubbing my tub.

Somehow you always end up scrubbing your tub at the oddest moments: your life has gotten out of control, you've run out of things to talk about, you can't concentrate on work, your house is a mess but you can't muster the energy needed to tidy up. Your whole situation is a disaster, but you're determined to find that one little thing you can still make pretty for posterity—and that thing is usually the bath. It's the most uncomplicated part of a house, a space without clothes or furniture or any of the intricate pleats and folds of the day-to-day. You just spray it down with water and scour until it shines. I was scrubbing my tub with a brush when I realized that it reminded me of something—and that something was a grave.

My dad once took me to visit his ancestral grave in Kagoshima. This was when I was still in kindergarten. For some reason it was just the two of us on that long ride through Kyūshū. I remember looking out the window at endless green fields, and being disappointed that the only animals I saw were cows. When I asked Dad what had happened to all the horses, he told me they'd been sent off to the war.

Every so often an announcement would blurt from the speakers, and everyone would rise from their seats and pull shutters down over the windows. These were wooden shutters, painted with brown varnish. The car would go weirdly dark, everyone sitting quietly until the next announcement, at which point we would get to our feet and push the shutters back up again, the car filling with light as everyone grumbled about the hassle. When I asked my dad what was going on, he told me that the windows had to be covered because we'd just gone by a secret military factory. There might be a spy on the train, he explained, and bad things would happen if they saw any factories. I glanced warily about, spooked by the word "spy," but everybody around me was calmly reading their newspapers. The train ride was a long one, and to pass the time, my dad made me little horses and giraffes from toilet paper he'd twisted into delicate little strings.

The cemetery was right next to a riverbed, in a meadow filled with tall, dead grass. Dad's younger brother and his uncle from Manchuria had both made the trip as well. The uncle was dressed in fancy white shoes and carried a camera, the shutter button of which he immediately began pressing. Realizing that this must be how photographs were made, I begged him to show me the pictures he was taking, right then and there, and was disappointed to learn that this was impossible. The only impression I had of the grave itself was that it seemed kind of pointless—unnecessary for life.

Later, when I was still a student in Tokyo, I went to Tama Cemetery with another uncle, from my mom's side of the family. He carried an urn filled with ashes. At some point this uncle had married into another family, but then he'd gotten divorced and devoted himself to bachelorhood. The ashes belonged to his faithful dog of a dozen years. He wanted to place the dog's ashes in the family grave, but Tama Cemetery had a rule against interring animals. So my uncle just went and jimmied open the grave himself. All it took was one good yank and the flagstone popped right out, revealing a small, square vault made of stone. Up until that moment, I hadn't realized that graves actually housed empty spaces beneath them.

The vault squirmed with stillness. My uncle placed one foot into this stillness, then turned and asked me to hold up the thick stone slab he'd just muscled open. I braced myself against the rock with all my might while he waded into the vault, placing his tiny urn on a stone shelf next to three larger ones. Then he began inventorying them aloud:

"Gosh, who's this again . . ."

This space would shortly be sealed off from the rest of the world. All I had to do was drop the flagstone, and my uncle would never reemerge. Of course the stone was fully propped up and showed no signs of tipping over, but I was still paranoid that I might accidentally knock it shut. When my uncle did finally climb back out, we lay the stone gently back over the grave, then sat on top of it to eat rice balls and tangerines.

I've visited other graves since then. Every once in a while, having somehow slipped free from the complicated morass of life, I'll find myself standing before a solitary headstone. I've even developed a certain fondness for graves. They're pleasant places—no wardrobes, no kitchens, no bookshelves. Every time I clean the bath, I daydream about them. They make me want to throw away my wardrobe and kitchen and bedroom and move into the tub. How simple would life be if we could throw away the tub as well and move into a spare, unassuming grave?

And then there was the time I actually saw a corpse inside a bath. This happened about a month after Dad passed, in the Nagoya apartment we abandoned in our rush to get my dad to Yokohama. We were so relieved to have safely moved him that we'd completely forgotten about the old place. The apartment was rent-controlled, and it felt like a shame to let it go, but none of us had any reason to go to Nagoya anymore, so my sister took care of the paperwork and we all gathered one last time to sort through the odds and ends of our estate.

Our folks had only taken a few changes of clothing when we'd whisked them off to Yokohama, and when we opened the door to their apartment it was exactly as we'd left it: filled with the stellar debris of our slowly spinning white dwarf. The old tube TV my little brother had bought for them. The oil paintings I'd done in high school. An ancient study desk we'd hauled all the way up from Ōita. I remembered that desk. Knife marks scarred its wooden top and the green paint on its sides. Looking closer, I saw that someone had carved the phrase "LIVE RIGHT" into it. We debated who the culprit was, and all agreed that the engraving was either the work of me or my little brother. It was definitely not something my older brother would do. We shared a laugh over this, but couldn't remember exactly who was responsible.

Thus we sifted through an apartment's worth of objects, each imbued with its own measure of history and significance. Almost everything had to be thrown out, and as we hauled this garbage out of the apartment, we reminisced about how people in the projects used to leave fully functional appliances out on the curb on garbage day.

The bath was the worst part. The entire bathing area had recently been remodeled to accomodate a genuine hinoki tub. Dad's first fall had taken place a mere six months after they'd installed it. The wood was practically brand new. We poked around, trying to figure out if it could be salvaged, but the tub wouldn't budge. It seemed like a terrible waste to throw out an unused bath, so we dropped in a hose and turned on the spigot, hoping to take it for one last spin. We were pretty much finished with the cleanup, so my brother and I went to the store for a six-pack and we all stretched out on the empty floor, listening to the sound of water as it gushed into the tub.

Normally when a bath fills up, the sound grows quieter as the water level approaches the nozzle of the hose. But for some reason the gushing of water in Dad's tub kept getting louder. After a while it started to sound like the hose might have slipped off the spigot and started spraying everywhere.

We went to the bathroom to investigate and found water pouring from the tub. Not overflowing from the top: it was coming out the sides. Little streams of water were spurting out between the vertical slats forming the ring of the tub. There were a dozen such planks, and now the whole thing looked like a fountain, streams radiating out every which way. It was as if a dozen different hoses had slipped off a dozen different spigots. I suddenly remembered that you had to leave a little water in the bottom of wooden bathtubs to keep them from drying out and warping. *It's all over*, I thought. I had a premonition, right then and there, that my dad would die. Of course my dad was already dead, so it was a weird premonition to have, but that's what happened. I had my premonition after the fact. There was no turning back, I realized in that moment. I recalled the look on his face as he lay in his casket. It had taken a couple days to arrange the wake, and by then his eyelids we'd so carefully closed had dried up, the whites of his eyes peeking through the gaps. There was no way to close those gaps anymore. They would just grow wider and wider until his eyeballs popped all the way out. The whites of a dozen eyeballs had appeared in the gaps of that dried-out tub. The whole mass of eyeballs stared at me. My dad had slipped through those cracks and vanished. Water continued to gush from the tub. It echoed off the walls and burrowed into my ears, where it clung like moss.

⦿⊙⦿

The slope is gentle, but eventually brings us to the top of the hill. Along the way, we've passed dozens of stonemasons, and now we're starting to see actual headstones on either side of the road. At last, the gate for Hachiōji Cemetery appears on our left. We've made it. But to our surprise, the large wrought-iron door is closed. Confused, I look at my wristwatch. 5:30 PM.

This comes as a bit of a shock. Here we are, having made the long trek from Mitaka, only to find that the show is already over. Which makes the cemetery sound like a movie or an art exhibition. A grave, however, can never really be "over."

Baba and I share a look. A somewhat defeated look.

Peering through the iron bars, we catch a glimpse of the graveyard, which stretches down a gentle incline. Orderly headstones punctuate the well-kept grass, blushing in the setting sun. It's a shade of pink that makes me nervous.

Between getting off to a slow start, disembarking at the wrong station, then stopping for sushi, we've arrived much later than expected. The sun is rapidly descending, pulling us deeper into the witching hour. At this point, it feels like our legs might very well melt away beneath us, dissolving into ghostly tails.

There's a small side door to the right of the gate. It's unlocked. We give it a push and it creaks open with an iron squeal. I feel as if I'm sneaking into a zoo through the back exit.

The cemetery is under construction. Only a handful of stragglers still wander the grounds. Eventually we locate the cemetery office. A lone bulb hangs above its door, glowing like a pale dumpling. Beneath the hastily fading sky, this wan light exacerbates my anxiety. I want to stop by the office and ask about plots, but the sun might set before we can see the grounds. Then again, if we walk around first, the office is liable to be closed by the time we get back. This is a municipal cemetery after all, and the people in the office are government employees. 5:30 is probably quitting time for them. And so we cast a regretful glance back at the grounds and slip into the office.

The office staff is sitting around sipping tea and chatting after a long day's work. It's a large space for such a small number of employees. The office must still be under construction, too. One of the workers notices us and stands up to greet us in a manner that wordlessly declares: *Wow, thanks for making the trip all the way out here!*

According to this kindly old clerk, all plots are a uniform four square meters in size and cost four hundred dollars up front, plus four dollars per year for upkeep. In order to apply for a spot, one must provide proof of residency in Tokyo and the remains of the deceased. Headstones may be in any style but must not exceed sixty centimeters in height and forty-two centimeters in width.

Sixty centimeters sounds awfully small to me. I turn and look out the window, noting the carefully arranged rows of identical graves. Something about the scene strikes me as lacking. I get that this is a cemetery built on the concept of equality, but something about it still feels fundamentally inadequate. Of course, I myself am just another member of the poor, faceless masses, so equality is the only option available to me—but that doesn't mean I have to like it. Even if I had the money to bury my dad beneath a meter-tall gravestone and flank it with gigantic camellias, they'd make me trim the stone down to sixty centimeters and pull up the flowers.

"The purpose of this cemetery is to provide burial plots for the citizens of Tokyo at minimum cost," the clerk explains. "If we don't place strict limits on size, patrons will feel obliged to spend more money on headstones. All it takes is one person putting up a big old tombstone for everyone else to feel like they have to do the same. And then there'd be no point in offering cheap plots in the first place."

It makes sense. I guess vanity and fashion follow us even to our graves.

"If you can afford a private plot, you're welcome to build as big a monument as you please. Why, just the other day I heard that some baseball player from the Giants just built a whole mausoleum for his parents right across the way in Tokyo Cemetery. They say it's as big and fancy as you might expect."

Across the street is a private cemetery full of condominium graves. We noticed headstones on that side of the street as we came up the hill, but we'd assumed they, too, were part of Hachiōji Cemetery. Apparently it's a totally separate outfit. This other cemetery is essentially laissez-faire: you can build as big a grave as your budget allows. I guess the little road that brought us here forms a sort of boundary between the graveyard of equality on the left, and the graveyard of capitalism on the right.

The clerk finishes up his spiel and we head out to survey the grounds, mindful of the setting sun. It's already growing dim and chilly, but the graveyard isn't nearly as spooky as we'd feared.

To me, a graveyard at night means ghosts. The mere presence of a grave nearby is enough to make the air swim with sinister shadows. Walking past a cemetery gate is about all my heart can handle. But this municipal graveyard, with its uniform headstones lined up like mahjong tiles, doesn't look like the sort of place where a ghost would choose to linger. It seems strange to say that there's no room for ghosts in a place as spacious as this, but it's true: the long, grassy incline of Hachiōji Cemetery is devoid of thickets, trees, or other shadowy areas. There's nowhere for a specter to suddenly emerge from, much less vanish back into. Even if a spirit wanted to haunt these grounds, there simply isn't any room to loom.

Most of the graves we walk by are shaped like matchboxes turned on end. Stylistically, they're going for a European look, but the result is just a smaller, chintzier version of the real deal. I've never cared for this sort of faux-foreign aesthetic, and the fact that everyone has opted for the same trendy design makes it feel even grosser. At least, that's my knee-jerk reaction. But then I remember that this uniformity isn't necessarily a question of choice. It's cemetery policy.

But I can't help but play the devil's advocate, here. Shouldn't the rules allow for a little memorial individuality? Part of the fun of visiting a cemetery is walking around and seeing all the different headstone flavors. Variety is the spice of death, and the markers here look so small and pathetic that you end up feeling sorry for whoever might be sleeping beneath them.

The sun has slipped behind the horizon, and the graveyard now stands before us bereft of both light and shadow. The sky maintains a vague glow, a lone star visible at its edge. Actually, I think it might be Jupiter. I start to feel embarrassed about getting stuck on the size and style of the gravestones—like some kind of business tycoon. It's just another mental hang-up of the living.

Maybe we're better off with wide-open graveyards like this: cemeteries without shadows, where specters aren't granted the luxury of looming. When you're dead, you're dead. There's plenty of business to take care of in the next life, so poking your nose back into this one is probably the last thing you want to do be doing.

And yet we, the living, are intent on creating graves exactly for this worst-case scenario. We don't really build graves for the dead; we do so for ourselves.

Off in the distance, the light is still on in the cemetery office. It's got to be past closing time by now, but they don't seem very strict about hours. Baba and I take a seat on the twilight lawn. The grass is soft and still faintly warm. It's not really dusk anymore; several stars are already starting to twinkle overhead. Though the sky is kind of black, it's also kind of blue, a blend of colors that has always appealed to me. It's the kind of color you see in your dreams. All the remaining light from the sky has been absorbed by the graveyard, giving it a similarly surreal glow. Distant things appear near, and near things seem far away. The stillness of the air feels straight out of a dream.

"Have you ever heard of gravistry?" I ask Baba.

"Gravistry?"

"It's like reading palms, except you read a person's grave."

"Ah, okay. Grave readings."

"Yeah. I read an interview in some weekly magazine with a guy who specializes in gravistry. Apparently his readings are always spot-on."

"A grave-reader, huh . . ."

"Yeah. You know how sometimes people have, like, a series of disasters? Their roof caves in, they get into a traffic accident, their house burns down or whatever. Well, eventually they find out that an ancestor's grave has been vandalized, or is in disrepair or whatever . . ."

"Sure. People love to tell stories like that. But you don't actually believe that stuff, right?"

"No, it's not that I believe it or anything. It's just that I can imagine there being some kind of correlation."

"I don't know, man. I get why people are into palm reading. But reading graves seems a little hokey because graves are, like, man-made objects."

"Apparently man-made objects have an aura of their own."

"They do? Says who?"

"Just bear with me for a moment. There's this fascinating part of the interview where the guy explains his process. He talks about how the typical grave is a three-story affair. The bottom part is a flat slab, then on top of that is a square stone base, and on top of that is a tall pillar-like headstone enscribed with the name of the deceased."

"Sounds about right."

"Well, according to gravistry, the top level represents the personality of the deceased, while the middle section represents their belongings, and the bottom represents whatever real estate they owned."

"Okay . . ."

"The thing is, you can't just have a huge flagstone at the base of your grave, or a really tall headstone without a base—you've got to maintain a certain balance between all three stones. And that's how a grave reader determines whether a grave has a good or bad aura."

"And this actually works?"

"I have no idea whether it works or not, but the theory is kind of cool."

"I just don't get it. I mean, I guess if there was some real-life correlation . . ."

"Think about it, though. None of the people applying for plots at this municipal cemetery—myself included—are very affluent. Most of us can only dream of ever owning real estate."

"Same here."

"I'm sure the rules of this particular cemetery aren't based on the principles of gravistry or anything, but if you think about it, none of these tombstones have a layer for real estate. None of them have a tangible personal property layer, either. All they have is that one lone headstone representing their personality."

"Ah . . ."

Everything around us has grown a shade darker. The grass has no discernible color, and the low-slung tombstones are increasingly indistinct. Rows of estate-less personalities stretch off into the distance, disappearing into the empty field beyond. The field in turn vanishes into the undeveloped hillside behind it, and the hillside fades into the darkness of night. The dead air around us seems to dip even further into the realm of dreams. Yet none of it feels spooky.

"Wouldn't it be freaky if you were conscious when you were born?"

"What?"

Baba looks startled.

"I just mean that it's probably better that we don't remember being born."

"Geez, you caught me off-guard with that one."

"We only become self-conscious slowly, over time, right? At the beginning of life, we're a blank slate. We gradually grow a consciousness and memories start to accrue. When we die, the same thing happens, just in reverse: our consciousness slowly slips away and we lose most of our memories. If we're lucky, we arrive at the same blank slate that we started out with."

"You mean going senile, right?"

"Yeah. The way I see it, senility is really important. There's something tragic about dying partway through life with your consciousness still intact. The most satisfying way to die has to be slipping back into infanthood and then vanishing the same way you arrived."

"But you can't experience satisfaction if you're dead."

"I disagree. I mean, dying is absolutely imperative to life, right? So there's got to be a satisfying way to die."

"Dying is absolutely imperative?"

"I mean, you have to be born in order to live, right? And you have to die in order to have lived. There's a certain temporal symmetry to life, so a really satisfying death must be one that manages to reflect and negate the life that preceded it."

"Hmm . . ."

"Apparently, all people experience death in the same series of stages."

"Stages?"

"According to psychological research, at least. When a patient is first informed that death is imminent, they go into shock. Then they question their diagnosis, or rage against the fates, or try to make deals with higher beings, or go into a severe depression, and so on. There are a number of different stages, each with its own accompanying emotions. But once you've passed through them all, you can settle down and accept death."

"Okay . . . But does this hold true for everyone?"

"Yeah—the study worked with a large sample of terminal patients, and everyone who made it to the final step had a similar experience. They say it's a lot like falling asleep. Patients who made it to the last step displayed a genuine sense of contentness, while those who only made it halfway suffered a lot in the end."

"Man, can we talk about something else please?"

"The fascinating part was that the people who said they'd worked hard and felt satisfied with their lives were able to get to that final stage of acceptance with relative ease, while those who grew up surrounded by material wealth or political connections had a really rough time and continued to reject the idea of death until the very end. A lot of them were in a bad state when they drew their last breath."

"I guess that makes sense. Some people are way too attached to worldly things. It's like they've got these big fishing weights on a line and are stuck pulling them around everywhere they go."

"Exactly. They've got too much of the world dragging around with them."

My back is starting to get cold. Even the grass has grown chilly to the touch. We've been sitting here for a while now, and the sky is almost black.

"Want to get out of here?" I say. "I wouldn't mind grabbing a drink at the station."

"Me neither."

We slowly get to our feet. I stretch, my knees and hips and shoulders popping. I'm already well into the latter half of my own life's symmetry, though one can never really see the larger outline of one's own life. It's like the outline of an ever-expanding universe.

From a distance, this place probably looks like a graveyard for unknown soldiers. I must have seen this in an American movie once: a vast cemetery of nameless graves. All you'd have to do is remove the names, and you'd have a graveyard for unknown citizens. I make up my mind then and there to apply for a plot.

The light is still on in the office. It's a very languid light. The least Baba and I can do is say goodbye before we leave. Once upon a time, the kind old man in the office would have been referred to as a "groundskeeper." And while the title of "cemetery groundskeeper" might conjure up the peg-legged hunchback from a gothic novel, this is a municipal cemetery, and the groundskeepers here are just regular old public servants.

Inside, we find the same elderly clerk enjoying a can of beer. He shoots us an embarrassed grin, and we smile back apologetically before slipping back out the door.

Once past the gates, we look across the street. There it is: the graveyard of condominiums. *Tokyo Cemetery.* The gate is closed, but the side entrance remains unlocked. Both graveyards have nearly identical gates.

"Well?"

Baba and I share a glance.

"Might as well, right?"

We give the side door a gentle shove, and just like its counterpart across the road, it squeals open on iron hinges.

The cemetery is dark—almost pitch black. Only a dim glow emanates through the murk from some distant source, lending faint shape to the faces of the headstones. The graves here are indeed the sort of gaudy structures that brazenly declaim "capitalism." It's so dark that all we can discern are outlines, but some are large enough to be categorized as obelisks. The triptych of personality, property, and real estate are on full display, in a variety of sizes and across a spectrum of styles. It feels as though the deceased themselves were standing right here, still alive.

Most of the graves are surrounded by small hedges and fences or flanked by decorative trees, weaving intricate tapestries of shadow in which almost anything could lurk. The inpenetrable penumbra of the unknowable. Every inch of the graveyard teems with ghosts. The souls of untold strangers wriggle about these lush shadows unimpeded, pressing in on us from all sides. We proceed slowly, tentatively, like a pair of rusty old robots. The darkness itself feels anxious, as though the shadows were crisscrossed with a million tiny wires, each connected to some invisible elsewhere. Our bodies press against these taut, black wires, tugging on the unknown. Through the wires, we feel the throbbing breath of darkness come vibrating back across our skin. This black breath thickens and swells, condensing in the shadows until all at once an inky mass thrashes up into the air. Baba and I freeze in our tracks. We see what looks like a thick, black newspaper flapping up into the sky. It circles low, twice, before hoisting its heavy body up and swooping off like a poorly made paper airplane. A crow, probably. A crow that sat poised in the shadows, breathing blackly. We're frozen in place and hurrying away at the same time. Capitalism, it turns out, has its own specters. Specters with fishing weights dragging behind them, their hooks sunk deep into the real estate of this world. It only stands to reason that they'd be loathe to leave it all behind.

Baba and I forget all about our creaky robot legs. The rust crumbles from our joints as we start walking—then full-on running—out of the graveyard of condominiums.

The street outside is well lit. On this side of the gate, it's just another evening. From time to time the lights of a passing car flash by on their way up the gentle slope. Everything, as far as we can tell, is just regular old everything.

the throes of home

MONTH A, DAY A (SUNNY)

"FUCK YOU, HOUSE!"

I throw my hands up. I've got forty-eight hours left until moving day, and it's starting to feel like the more stuff I pack, the more embroiled it all gets. I'm sick of it.

So I whip the door to one side with a rattle:

RATTLE-RATTLE-RATTLE!

But I'm probably just imagining the rattle because that's how the front door worked in my childhood home. Or maybe I'm copping this sound from the movies. Doors don't really rattle anymore. Nowadays, they only click and swing:

Click, swish.

It's a hinged door. You have to twist a little round knob to open it. All modern condos and housing developments have doors like this. Apartment complexes, too. Even the old wooden tenement I'm renting features a hinged door; it's not about to do any rattling. All you get is:

Click, swish.

Which is a little off-putting—especially at times like these. Times when you want to yell, "Fuck you, house!" and go storming out. Times when you need to grab the front door and whip it to the side with a tremendous rattle as if sweeping away all the droopy, clingy things around you.

"I'm outta here!"

RATTLE-RATTLE-RATTLE!

You need some rattling if you want to leave your house with any aplomb. The whole sentiment falls flat when you have to reach out, grasp a doorknob, twist, then swing the door open.

Click, swish.

"Pardon me," you feel like saying. "I'm stepping out, but I won't be terribly late. Yes, I promise to drink in moderation. You take care, too, dear. I love you."

Then you pull the door shut behind you and step out onto the sidewalk, slinking off to go help with the neighborhood litter patrol or whatever. That's how hinged doors make you feel.

So now I don't know what to do with myself. I could have left with the momentum of a resounding "fuck you," but this door has denuded my "fuck you" of all conviction. Who knew that a door could be so problematic?

I stop and look back at the door. It stands there, primly closed. Something about its primness feels almost derisive. That's when I remember: hinged doors can be slammed.

Fighting couples do this all the time:

"What's your problem?" shouts your spouse.

"My problem?" you bellow, leaping to your feet and throwing on your coat. "You're my goddamn problem!"

"Have it your way!" your spouse hollers as you stomp wildly out of the room.

But when you open the front door, all you get is a gentle click and swish:

Click, swish.

Which clearly isn't going to cut it. That sound will only drag you right back into your daily rhythm. So you toss off some final invective—the meanest thing you can think of: "Asshole!" "Freak!" "Chronically constipated!"

And then you slam the door behind you with a resounding bang:

BANG!!!

Which at least maintains a semblance of form. You thrust your chin out and throw your shoulders back, trying to keep that "fuck you" feeling as you stride down the street, kicking at an empy can:

Clatter, clatter, clatter . . . That's it. That's what I should do.

So I go back to the house. I go back to the house and turn the knob. The door swings open with a swish. I stand there for a moment, running my fingertips along the edge of the open door, thinking. Just thinking.

This rental unit has stood here for some forty years. The door itself must be equally old. Its hinges are nearly rusted through, the knob resting loose in the latch. I feel like one good slam might send the whole thing clattering to the floor. And then I'd be too worried about the door to yell "fuck you" and storm away. I'd have to check and make sure everything was still working, then gently close it all over again:

Swish, click.

At which point I'd probably only have enough momentum left to go to the post office for a book of stamps. Which would be missing the point entirely. The word "fuck" in "fuck you, house!" would begin to sound like—I don't know—like a mere rhetorical flourish. And that's a problem. Using "fuck" as a rhetorical flourish is pretty much sacrilege.

So I'm stuck. I squat down right there in the doorway, rest my chin on one fist, and begin thinking. A moment ago I'd summoned the courage to tell this house to fuck off, but thanks to one dumb door I can't seem to see the sentiment through to its conclusion. Had this been a regular sliding door that rattled open, I'd already be barreling briskly through town, dealing with whatever important business I felt like dealing with. But thanks to a couple rickety hinges, I'm stuck squatting on the stoop.

I guess you can't take architecture with a grain of salt. The design of a single entryway can make a huge difference in a person's life. It's kind of scary.

I crouch down. Then I unfurl my body and stretch flat on my back. My feet, still in their sandals, jut out of the doorway. They're the only part of me exposed to the outside world. And while my feet feel lovely, I can sense the entire house behind my back, simmering like a stew. My worldly possessions are all massed together in a tangle, each item with its own invisible network of threads leading off to other things: a sweater entwined with a memory; a piece of dinnerware snarled up with the curbside garbage; an old book mixed in with the recycling. I've been trying to snip my way through these strands, but with every chop I make they grow back twofold. My apartment looks like a radio I tried to take apart and couldn't figure out how to reassemble. So I lie flat on my back in the foyer, threads still yanking at my head, feet jutting out of the house.

The wind wiggles its way into the gap between my sandals and feet. I feel like I'm lying on a beach with my toes in the ocean. The stoop is the tideline. Salt air blows over my body and into the apartment. Beneath my legs, insects move slowly over the sand. This is one of those gentle beaches that stay shallow way out into the ocean, even as the tide rolls in and out. Which explains all the old shoes and sandals that have washed up here by the door. And the broken umbrella. The rust on my doorknob is probably due to the salty sea breeze.

The coastal postman stops by. His shadow falls over me as I lie there on the beach. Parking his red bicycle on the sand, he says:

"Registered mail for you. Can I get your stamp?"

It's the paycheck for my weekly painting class. I reach back with one hand and stretch into the hallway, twisting my body until I feel my fingers on the latch of a drawer, where I fumble around until I find my dirty old stamp.

"Thanks!" I say, foisting my stamp into the air. The postman takes it from me and presses it onto a complicated form. Then he whips off the top copy and hands me the envelope along with my stamp.

"You're welcome, sir."

"Cheers," I say as the postman pedals creakily off into the sea. The sun is falling on my face again. I drop the envelope onto the sand and stretch back out on the shoreline. The breeze blows a snarl of sea grass across the marge. Then the wind stops all at once, the sun growing warm on my face. It really is a lovely day.

A neighbor strolling down the beach sneaks a peek at my sunbathing body as they pass. Their peeking, however, quickly escalates into a full-blown gawk. I can feel their disapproving gaze on my body, and open my eyes to glare back only to find that this isn't a neighbor at all: it's good old Memori. Memori used to be a student of mine.

"What's wrong, Teach? Low blood sugar or something?"

"No," I groan.

"You fall down . . . ?"

"Nope. I lay down."

"Why would you lie down in the doorway?"

"This is a beach. I'm napping."

"Okay . . . Hm. Uh, so how's the packing going?"

"Packing, right . . . To be honest, there's no way I'm ever going to get this all packed up. The whole house—it's just boiling back there like a stew."

"Huh?"

"All my crap. It's been reduced to a stewy ooze. We're gonna have to scoop it up with a ladle."

"Well, you asked me to come help, so here I am. But if you're already in that kind of mood . . ."

Memori has seen me through two moves. The first time was back when he was a student, and I was stuck in the superglue of a seven-year marriage, squirming and writhing, incapable of moving forward or backward. I wasn't even capable of moving laterally. By the time it was all over, I was as tired and worn down as a stripped screw. It was one of those moves where all you have left is your decision to move.

I made that decision one day while walking out of a coffee shop. Out of the blue, I asked the woman with me if she wanted to start a relationship. She was working at a canned food company. Like Memori, she had once been a student of mine. We were meeting for the first time in years—not because I harbored any special feelings for her, but because I needed help with some design-related work. It was probably because I didn't have any special feelings for her that I was able to bring up the prospect of a relationship as if it were a joke. And she, for her part, played it off like a joke. The day was overcast, threatening rain at any moment. It felt like a movie: the two of us standing in front of the train station, people walking back and forth in front of us. Even the way she smiled was straight out of the pictures. But there were shades of discomfort to that smile, as well. Walking home afterwards, I realized I was still carrying the envelope full of materials I'd meant to give her. I had left home wearing only a pair of beach sandals, and went wandering about town like that until I found myself pounding on a friend's door. I remember my friend staring at my naked feet like I was nuts.

It took a week to find a new place to live, and Memori agreed to drive the U-Haul. He parked right in front of my old apartment. It had only been my "old" apartment for about a week, the door still sticky from seven years' worth of superglue. I yanked at it. It took a little elbow grease, but the door eventually popped open and I began lugging my stuff out without a word. Memori followed suit, likewise wordless. A pair of eyes, bloodshot with drugs and alcohol, followed us from inside the apartment. My own eyes, worn down like stripped screws, stared vacantly back. The bloodshot eyes went to the dresser, pulled out a pair of matching sweaters, and began dumping things into the hallway. Memori and I silently gathered these things up and carried them to the U-Haul. By the time we drove away, I was so emotionally drained that I felt mummified. We were a full two hours late returning the truck, and I ended up shelling out for an extra day. I tried to play the whole thing off as a joke, referring to it as "Operation Entebbe."

I spent a year in my new apartment with the woman from the canned food company. After that, we ran out of words. There were no bloodshot eyes this time, though. Nobody had squeezed out any superglue. The lid had been left on the tube. It was like walking out of a movie. The images on the screen stopped moving and then the curtains swung shut.

Once again I asked Memori to drive the U-Haul for me. He immediately acquiesced, as though it went without saying. I slipped silently out of the apartment, and when I returned, half the stuff that had occupied it was already gone. I was the last one to leave that time. I remember sitting down among the remaining boxes and thinking that I wanted a cigarette for the first time in years.

"People move for a lot of different reasons," Memori is still talking. "This time it's because your lease is up?"

"People get divorced for a lot of reasons, people go to war for a lot of reasons . . ."

I pull my feet back inside the foyer. I can feel the cold water dripping off them after their long dip in the ocean.

"Moving," I venture, "is really radical."

"Hmm . . ." Memori considers this. I can tell he's trying to think of some pithy reply, but can't quite pin down what I mean by "radical." At last he asks: "You mean 'radical' as in extremist radical?"

"Yeah. I mean, there's something really radical about the idea of a house."

"A house," he echoes. "There's something radical about the idea of a house . . ."

"I mean, a house is real estate. You can't move a house—that's the whole point."

"Real estate . . . Okay . . ."

"Yeah, it's stuck in the ground like a thumbtack. Everybody's walking around dragging this long string behind them, and the other end of the string is nailed to the ground by a gigantic thumbtack. A house is basically just a thumbtack."

"Thumbtacks *are* pretty radical."

"And sometimes you have to move your thumbtack! So you pop it out and it goes rolling around on the floor. And an uprooted thumbtack is a dangerous thing."

"You might step on it. Get jabbed."

"Yeah, the fundamental desire of a thumbtack is to jab something."

"When are you moving again?"

"In two days."

"Oh shit, I have to work . . ."

"Don't worry about it. I've got plenty of help."

"Sorry, Teach."

"No problem. This time, it's going to be a lot easier. Emotionally."

"Emotionally, eh?"

"Yeah. Emotionally."

My legs are starting to feel stiff. I shake them out, stomp the ground, then kick them up in the air and slap the soles of my sandals together—*clap, clap, clap*. But it feels as if my feet are clapping for someone else.

MONTH 8, DAY 8 (SUNNY)

I move my house. There are quite a few boxes. More than quite a few—an overwhelming number. An overwhelming number of things to carry. My Nikon FE, for example. And my Rollei 110. And my Olympus XA. Actually, my cameras make up only a fraction of the stuff I own. The rest is all junk and refuses to decrease in volume no matter how much of it I pack. For example, I'll put one of my Nikon bodies in a box only to find all my Nikon lenses still lying about. Seriously, though: the cameras are only a fraction of my stuff, the rest of which is all junk and refuses to decrease in volume.

I have to hit up the grocery store for more boxes. It's the same place I always go to—the green grocer where I buy my peppers and daikons. Sometimes I buy onions and potatoes there, too.

A clerk is standing outside in a baseball cap, breaking down boxes. He's glancing in my direction. I think he recognizes me.

"Hey," I say. "I was wondering if I could take twenty boxes off your hands."

"That's a lot of boxes."

"I got a lot of junk."

"You moving?"

"Yep. Just over to the west side of the station."

"That's a mighty short move."

"Yep. But I still gotta box everything up."

"Boxes, right . . . Well, we've got plenty of boxes. How many did you need again?"

"Around twenty."

"Lemme see what we have . . ."

The clerk disappears into the back of the store, then comes back with a stack of neatly folded boxes.

GUNMA SPINACH

GUNMA PREFECTURE BUSINESS FEDERATION

The bottoms of the spinach boxes are stained dark green and muddy. They're straight from the farm. They're even stamped with a grange seal. Spinach. I love spinach.

CHOICE CABBAGE
HŌYA CITY AGRICULTURAL COOPERATIVE
TOKYO BUSINESS FEDERATION

I love cabbage, too. It's good minced; it's great pan-fried; it's delicious pickled in red miso. You can even boil it and make cabbage rolls.

HIGHLAND LETTUCE
NAGANO PREFECTURE

Lettuce. You can't cook lettuce.

KAŌ WATERMELON
KUMAMOTO SELECT 2-3 L

Watermelon isn't really part of a meal. Fruits are dessert. It seems kind of weird that they sell desserts at a green grocer.

I pile twenty boxes onto the back of my bike and pedal home. Then I reassemble the boxes, secure their bottoms with packing tape, and start tossing stuff in. Before I know it, they're full of junk. But nothing about my apartment has changed. I don't have nearly enough boxes.

So I head back to the grocer.

"Hey, I was wondering if I could get twenty more boxes."

"You need more boxes?"

"I've got more junk."

"Really?"

The clerk stops what he's doing. This time he's sorting vegetables. I can almost see the image forming in his head: a never-diminishing mountain of junk. A junk black hole. Or the opposite of a black hole—a white hole.

"Right now," he peers into the rear storeroom, "we've only got half a dozen. There'll be more in the afternoon if you come back then."

Looks like I'm stuck.

Later in the day, a man from the moving company comes by to give an estimate. After carefully reconnoitering my apartment, he says:

"Hmmm . . ."

Something about this "hmmm" makes me nervous.

"How many more boxes do you think I'll need?" I ask. "Another twenty or so . . . ?"

"Forty," he says, a cigarette dangling from his lips. "Maybe more."

Smoking isn't allowed in the apartment, but I'm in no position to argue.

I can't believe it. I mean, it's my own junk, so I have to believe it, but I've already packed twenty-two boxes and the thought of forty more is downright depressing. Houses are the worst. To think a tiny space like this could suck up so much stuff—it's gross. I just want to wash my hands of the whole thing. Which is what moving is, essentially: washing your hands of an entire home.

Moving day rolls around. The movers park a two-ton truck right there on the thoroughfare and immediately start hauling boxes out of my apartment. They look professional. I ended up with ninety-six boxes. The green grocer didn't have enough, so I hit up the pharmacy, too. I also went to the art supply store. I'm pretty sure I rustled up every last empty box in town.

The whole process made me feel dirty and ashamed, like a high school kid soliciting magazine subscriptions. Most of the boxes came from the grocer, but a lot of them—boxes for tomatoes and cucumbers in particular—were too shallow to use. The best boxes for moving are cabbage boxes. Followed by bok choy, then lettuce, then spinach.

Still, ninety-six is a pretty ridiculous number of boxes—just four away from a solid century! If you count the books bundled up with twine and the paper bags filled with odds and ends, it actually comes out to more than a hundred. Do I really need all this . . . stuff? Surely a man can survive on the contents of a box or two, right? The whole situation disgusts me. So I stand there, basking in disgust. The sheer constipation of all my possessions makes me feel like a cow's lethargic digestive tract, or a bag of kitchen garbage that you keep forgetting to take out on trash day. I actually wince.

The movers get right to it. One by one my boxes are lugged out and stacked in the bed of the truck, starting from the front.

I can tell that the movers are real professionals by the way they leverage every available bit of space, slipping boxes and bags into the complicated gaps between desks and chairs. Everything fits together like a puzzle. There's such a perfectly interlocked singularity of stuff inside the shell of that truck that I wonder how they'll ever get any of it back out.

It takes two trips to move everything. On the second trip, they actually have to stack stuff on top of the truck, its perfect rectangle interrupted by the odd angles of my junk as it rumbles down the road.

I stay behind to give the empty apartment a final scrub. The dirt left in the wake of my worldly possessions is much coarser than the dust I've become accustomed to living with. A cobweb dangles like a tattered curtain from the wall where my bookshelf used to be. Mold blooms from the stucco beneath the window where my dresser once stood. I guess it had been leaking this whole time. Mold had been feeding on the grimy rain, sketching black patterns in the plaster. I feel like I've got one of those dental mirrors in my mouth and am examining the backsides of my own incisors.

I start wiping everything down. This empty house bereft of possessions—does it even count as a house anymore? My hands stop cleaning mid-scrub. I will never sleep here again. I'm scrubbing an anonymous room. Purged of my stewing morass of possessions, this erstwhile home is now just a clean, empty space.

"Not too shabby . . ."

I pause again. Through fresh eyes, this place doesn't look half bad. I wouldn't mind living in a big, empty room like this. Maybe I should give it a second chance. Now that it's empty, I feel like the apartment and I could work things out.

I sit down in the middle of the floor. The tatami mats are completely bare, revealing a whole new side to themselves. It's like touching the skin of a stranger for the first time. Stroking the surface of the floor through the dust, I remind myself that the moment I make this my home again, things will start sticking to all its exposed surfaces. Used books, magazines, scrapbooks, cameras, the lenses belonging to my cameras—they will all affix themselves to its walls like barnacles on the hull of a ship. Possessions, I realize, are barnacles. A house's walls are a hull.

I set my scrubbing hand back in motion and finish the job. After giving the hallway one last wipe, I whisk the dirty rag up off the floor and hold it aloft, letting it dangle in the air as I strut straight out the door, not even bothering to lock up. There's nothing back there to lock up anyway. Nothing but empty space. I take my time walking toward my new house, the rag still dangling from my hand. My friends are probably in my new room, unloading all the boxes. I bet the boxes are already open and my stuff is slithering out, dazed from the journey, glancing shiftily about. My new room is in the throes of becoming a home. The thumbtack that was rolling around on the floor has been stuck into a new location and is swiftly being pounded into place. But for the moment I'm in an empty, liminal space. I'm walking through this emptiness, rag in hand.

I arrive at my new house. It's new to me, but the building itself is rather old, with pit toilets instead of flushable ones. The kitchen sink is tile rather than stainless steel, and the cracks in the grout have been sealed up with cement. It probably leaks a little. The front door isn't a hinged one: it's a sliding wooden door—one that rattles open. The whole entryway feels firm and masculine. I slide the door open. It makes me feel like a man. A real old-fashioned bloke, single-minded to a fault, who says what he means and means what he says, literal and sincere but not afraid of a good fight—that's the kind of asshole I feel like as I rattle the door open. There's already a good stew brewing inside. The stuff from my old house is piled high in a long mountain range. Tectonically speaking, these mountains are still mid-formation—I can feel them bubbling up all around me. The boxes at their peaks have begun to blow their lids, scattering my possessions about. They pile up here and there, sticking to the corners of the room. The things we own really are barnacles. The walls of my new house are slowly moving toward me, a hull below water. A home is forming right before my eyes.

MONTH C, DAY C (SUNNY)

Today I'm going to buy a gutter. Two gutters. I feel like in this day and age, a gutter is the most radical purchase one can make.

Sure, buying a Nikon F3 might make some people feel like they're on top of the world, but if you ask me, that's already been done. Purchasing a camera is played out. We already know that buying a camera is going to make you feel like a million bucks. The whole Nikon F3 thing feels a bit hackneyed at this point.

Nowadays it's all about gutters. Going out to buy a gutter on a beautiful day. Just moseying over to the hardware store in the sun and purchasing a couple of gutters. Sure, you could always buy them on a cloudy day, but the clouds are going to put you under a lot of pressure to get those gutters up. Seriously, it looks as though it might start raining any minute now. And that's not ideal. The most radical thing to do is to buy your gutters on a dry, cloudless day and to take your sweet time nailing them to the eaves.

I call up Memori. He's renowned for wearing toilet sandals around town. Well, maybe "renowned" is an overstatement.

"Hey, I'm buying some gutters today."

"Um, hello?"

"Hey, I'm buying some gutters today."

"Oh, it's you. What's up?"

"What's up. Hey—I'm buying some gutters today."

"Gutters?"

"Yeah, you busy?"

"Not really, but . . ."

"Because I'm gonna go buy some gutters."

"Gutters. Okay. For your roof?"

"Yeah. I'm gonna buy two of them. Want to come?"

"Sure, that's fine and swell—but why? What, are you gonna, like, hang them from your eaves . . . ?"

"Well, yeah. That's what gutters are for. What's wrong with you?"

"Okay, gotcha. It was just a little abrupt, so I thought maybe you didn't actually need gutters. Like, maybe you were just buying them on impulse. Which would be weird."

"No way, man. Who the hell buys gutters on impulse?"

"Yeah, that would be crazy."

"Well, I don't know if I'd call it 'crazy.' It's the kind of thing an artist would do. Buying gutters on impulse would be pretty blatant art. And that kind of shit is played out."

"Played out?"

"Yeah, played out. It's been done. The whole art thing is a little played out at this point if you ask me."

"Okay . . . ?"

"It's already old news. Especially contemporary art—that's the oldest news of all."

"Contemporary art. Got it."

"So listen: I just moved."

"Yeah, I know."

"And my new place has these eaves that hang out over the garden. But there aren't any gutters, and the rain just kind of dribbles off the roof in one spot."

"Your new place has a garden?"

"Yeah, a garden. I have a garden. These days it's all about gardens."

"Oh dear. Gardens."

"Yeah, I even planted some grass. From here on out, it's all about having grass."

"From here on out, eh?"

"Yeah. I've got a little porch that looks out over the garden. And the eaves hang over this porch."

"You're renting a whole house?"

"Of course it's a whole house. These days you don't want a half-house, or a third-of-a-house, or one of those tenth-of-a-house houses—what are they called—condominiums?"

"Come on. You know what they're called."

"Ha ha, yeah. But still, the most avant-garde purchase you can make these days is a gutter. A gutter for the eaves above your porch. There's no point in buying gutters if you live in a condo."

"Man, you really have it out for condos, don't you."

"Not really. I don't discriminate. I'm not harboring an anti-condo agenda or anything. I just find something inadequate about the whole concept . . ."

"Sure, but condo owners are free to walk over to the hardware store and buy gutters same as you."

"Of course they can. But why would they? That would be like buying a rearview mirror when you don't own a car."

"Hmmm . . ."

"Which, anyway, like I said, I've moved, and my eaves hang out over my yard, and the rain dribbles off them in this one spot."

"Okay . . . ?"

"It's a big problem! I can hear the rain going 'drip, drop, drip, drop . . . '"

". . . ?"

"And after it's dribbled off the eaves, it makes a little ditch right in the middle of the grass."

"I imagine it does."

"Exactly! All those raindrops keep making a ditch in the same spot. And when I fill the ditch back up, the rain just makes another one all over again."

"And for some reason this really bothers you?"

"Yeah. The drops keep splashing into the same puddle, and the ditch keeps getting deeper and deeper, and everything feels all gross and wet, like when it rains and you forget to bring in your laundry."

"Ah, I'm with you there. You can't just leave your laundry out like that."

"Yeah, exactly. But once the rain starts to form a ditch, it's easy to stop caring. Like when the corner of a rug starts to curl up and you try to straighten it out at first, but eventually you give up and start stepping on it, which only aggravates the crease, so you end up resigning yourself to living with a dog-eared rug."

"I guess I know what you mean . . ."

"Well my grass is this rug, and there's a ditch forming in it."

"Yeah, you've told me all about it."

"I guess condo owners don't have to worry about ditches."

"Now we're back on the condos."

"The point is that I need to put gutters on my eaves, and today is the day I purchase them. Two gutters, to be precise. Wanna come?"

Memori shows up that afternoon. He's wearing a grey jumpsuit and one of those hats that electricians wear. And he's sporting the kind of sandals that you wear in restrooms—the floppy rubber kind.

"Afternoon!"

"Well, if it isn't Monsieur Memori. And you're wearing bathroom sandals again!"

Memori was running around in these same sandals during one of our extracurricular softball games. We were all like: "Hey Memori! Don't you have any shoes? You're wearing the sandals from the bathroom!" And he was like, "No way, these are mine!" And someone said: "Wait, those are yours? I thought they were for the bathroom! I've been wearing them whenever I go to take a piss!" And someone else was like: "Me too! Me too!" The restroom at our school was notoriously filthy, and since Memori left his grody old sandals lying around, everyone just assumed they were the restroom sandals and would change into them whenever they used the urinal. But that didn't stop Memori from using those same sandals to sprint from first base to second base, then from second to third, and finally home for an infield home run.

"It's a good look, right?" Memori says. "Since we're shopping for gutters, I thought I'd coordinate my style."

"I like it. From here on out, it's all about the gutter look. Gutter style."

"Ha ha, gutter style. Oh, hey, is this your garden? Not bad, Teach. I dig it—you're really moving on up. Now I see what you mean . . ."

"You see? Over there! The rain runs off the roof right over there—see how the grass looks like it's been mangled or something?"

"Here?"

“Now look straight up—see the eave right above that spot?”

“The eave, okay. So water comes running off right here. Gotcha. This most definitely calls for gutters.”

“Vamanos.”

So we head out to buy gutters, making our way down quiet afternoon streets. Three little toddlers are waddling about. Three corresponding mothers stand to one side, chatting: *Well, at our house we make a point of* . . . It’s a crisp day, the sky endlessly blue.

“What a beautiful day,” Memori says.

“It’s perfect. This here is gutter weather.”

“Yes indeed.”

“You can’t beat weather like this for putting up gutters. From here on out.”

“From here on out. Right.”

“Yessiree. With weather like this you can take your sweet time putting up gutters. Hang them nice and careful-like. You wouldn’t want to hang gutters on a cloudy day. Can you imagine?”

“Clouds, yeah . . .”

“And if it’s actually raining—forget about it. Putting up gutters on a rainy day is out of the question.”

“Man, in the rain? Putting up gutters in the rain sounds nuts.”

“It wouldn’t be nuts, per se.”

“Imagine being up on the roof in the pouring rain, trying to put up gutters. Sounds nuts to me.”

“Doesn’t sound nuts to me. Gutters in the rain.”

“Gutters in the rain . . .”

"That's poetry or something. It's contemporary art. Totally hackneyed, in other words."

"Played out."

"Completely played out. From here on out."

"From here on out. Right."

Walking slowly toward the hardware store, we cast furtive glances at the blue sky above us. Below the blue of the sky are red tile roofs, at the ends of which are little eaves. And lining these little eaves are gutters. Memori and I extend our furtive glances and casually appraise these gutters. Most are grey or brown with rounded bottoms. A few are square with flat bottoms. The square ones seem a little pretentious.

"What do you think about the square ones?" I ask.

"The square ones? I dunno. They seem kinda . . . tacky?"

"Exactly. It's like their owners are trying to show off via their gutters. Who does that?"

"Seriously—who does that?"

"Hey, look. That house doesn't have *any* gutters at all."

"Really? Oh yeah, you're right. But there's a pipe running down from that one corner."

"Well, I'll be. The gutters must be built right into the eaves, I reckon."

"I reckon you're right. Must be one of those prefabricated houses."

"A factory home. With prebuilt eaves. Fully integrated gutters."

"Integrated, right."

"Don't know if I care for them."

"Definitely don't care for them."

"Why would you hide your gutters away when gutters are precisely the kind of thing you should be showing off?"

"Exactly. If you've got it, flaunt it. Nothing to be ashamed of here."

"Nothing to be ashamed of at all. I bet the people who live there think they're too cool for gutters. I bet they put on pedantic airs and perorate about how gutters are primitive and campy, how they bring down the whole aesthetic of Japanese architecture."

"Screw those people, man."

We find ourselves growing terse. We want to avert our eyes from this house with hidden gutters. We feel like it's turned its nose up at us, stolen our thunder. Here we had gotten ourselves all amped up about gutters, and now this newfangled prefabricated home has rained on our parade. Could it be that gutters are considered tacky?

"What a nice day it is," I say.

The clear, hard image of a gutter that I was holding in my mind has started to soften. My original intention was to purchase the most baroque-looking gutter I could find, but now I'm feeling a little self-conscious.

We arrive at the hardware store. The gutters are leaning up against the wall outside, next to ladders, iron pipes, and laundry poles. As expected, they only come in grey or brown. All are plastic. I choose the more humble grey—with rounded bottoms, of course. The most commonplace kind. Stamped on their sides is:

TAKIRON 100 TJ

"From here on out," I say, "it's all about the Takiron 100 TJ."

"That's right—the Takiron 100 TJ is where it's at," Memori laughs. "From here on out."

We carry the gutters home on our shoulders stretcher-style, slapping at their shiny plastic bellies as we walk. I've never been fond of plastic as a material, but this particular polymer feels pleasantly soft. The gutters have a radius of 50 millimeters and are . . . let's see . . . 3800 millimeters long. Stretched out between us, they wiggle slightly.

The toddlers are still wobbling about in the street. Their moms are still standing around chatting: *Well, at our house we . . .* The sky has been blue all morning, and now the sun sits right at its apex, bright rays caressing the smooth surface of my new gray gutters—a truly radical scene.

We set about hanging the gutters as soon as we get back. My new house actually has two separate porches facing the garden, each with its own eave. I want to hang gutters on both eaves so they can channel the rain to the middle, where I plan to lay down gravel. That way I won't need a pipe to guide the water to the ground. Even with gutters, the prettiest solution is always the most minimal one.

We hang the gutters. I stand up on a chair and touch the eaves of my new house for the very first time. They feel sunny and great. These are the first gutters I've ever bought. Brand-new gutters. I imagine all the neighborhood housewives noticing me from their second-floor windows. They throw down their sewing and exclaim:

"Well I'll be—brand-new gutters!"

"Look at those lovely Takiron 100 TJs!"

"That's the brand I've always wanted."

"We went with the Benz, but these days I hear it's all about Takiron gutters."

"We decided on a Rolex, but everybody says Takirons are where it's at."

"Well, in our home, we have Rémy Martins, but Takirons are the real deal."

"I hear they've got a 50-millimeter radius!"

"The grey ones are just divine."

"Absolutely fahhhbulous."

Imagining all this makes me self-conscious. I sneak a glance up at the second-floor window of my neighbor's house. Their windows are demurely closed, too shy to even venture a peek.

"That side needs to go up a little," Memori says, standing across the yard to scrutinize the gutter's tilt. I climb up on the chair and make a subtle adjustment. "It's gotta slope slightly to one side for the water to flow out properly."

"Sure," I say, "I get it, the water needs an incline to run down. But I don't want it to look crooked, either."

"Okay . . ."

"There should be just enough tilt for the water to start beading up at the bottom, then change its mind at the last minute and roll five centimeters in the right direction—that's how much slope you want."

"That's how much you need. From here on out."

We finish hanging the gutters and drink beers on the patio. Perfect blue continues to spread across the sky. My gutters wait in anticipation under this unimpugnable blue: slightly sloped, slick and new, never once so much as wetted. Something about their gentle tilt seems incredibly expectant—madly radical.

MONTH D, DAY D (SUNNY)

For a while I was convinced that a gutter was the most radical purchase a person could make. But over the past few days I've begun to think that a doorknob might be an even more radical investment.

It's not often that you get the chance to buy a doorknob, especially in this day and age. I mean, sure, you're welcome to head over to the hardware store and buy yourself a doorknob if you have some extra cash lying around. But buying something you have no practical need for sounds like regular old contemporary art . . . What's that? You say this whole train of thought is played out?

Anyway, my point is that the back door leading into my kitchen is extremely stubborn. The knob refuses to turn, no matter how hard you twist it. This isn't even a matter of torque, per se—the entire door is glued to its frame with cooking grease. It's like the last tenant never cleaned. He probably thought cleaning was a waste of time. Grease just kept popping out of his stir-fries and hot pots, building up on the door until its entire surface was as sticky as a roach trap. And now opening it requires throwing your whole body against it, which makes you lose your balance and grab the doorframe for support—at which point you're stuck there like a dopey cockroach, trapped by your own kitchen. It's a pretty crazy kitchen.

The doorknob was already dysfunctional when the realtor first brought me to see the place. This door: it's like it doesn't even want to be a door. Not only is the doorknob stuck, but the key won't turn. It slides into the lock fine; it just doesn't turn.

The realtor was already in a bad mood when she showed me the place.

"Well, sumvabitch . . . This lock . . . I meant to tell the landlord . . . sum-va-bitch. Sum . . . Sum . . . sumvabitch."

She just kept saying "sumvabitch."

Eventually the key turned with a "pop." Even a broken old latch like this will give up and unlock if you clamp both hands around it and throw all your weight in one direction.

The realtor had the distinct aura of a married women. She was wearing a long tunic with plastic sandals. A necklace peeked out from behind her collar, and she was extremely vocal. Every time she got worked up she would let out this same "sumvabitch."

The lock itself was pretty old and probably rusted all the way through, but I guess even a rusty old lock will turn if a realtor yells "sumvabitch" at it enough. And so the lock did open that one time. It would never do so again.

"I can't imagine Mr. Kawamura going through the trouble of opening this door every day . . ."

Apparently the previous tenant's name was Mr. Kawamura.

The realtor brushed her hands off, held out a twine loop with two keys on it, and said:

"At any rate, here are the keys. I don't know how useful they'll be."

The keys hung from the twine, jangling like a pair of Popper Knockers. To me, they were just pointless pieces of metal. I had no use for them. I just stared at where they dangled from the realtor's fingers.

"Here . . ." she said again.

She seemed to be having a hard time figuring out what to say next.

"Um . . ." she said.

A "here" followed by an "um." I gave up and took the keys, letting them dangle from my own fingers like a dirty rag. The realtor averted her gaze and grasped the doorknob.

"Anyway," she said.

I had no idea what this "anyway" referred to, but it was clearly meant to direct conversation away from the lock and toward the door. Except that the door still wouldn't budge. The bolt was open, and all that remained to do was turn the knob and pull the door open. But the knob refused to turn. It moved a little, wiggling around in its socket like a loose screw, but wouldn't actually turn. It was stuck. The door looked like it was glued to its frame.

"Well . . . hmm . . ."

The realtor grasped the brass knob with both hands and tried twisting it to the right.

"Well . . . hmm . . ."

Then she tried turning to the left.

"Well . . . hmm . . ."

She planted her feet and began digging in. With both hands on the knob, she again threw her weight to the right and then to the left. From behind, it looked like she was trying to pull a giant spear out of her belly. Her plastic sandals bit into her heels; her necklace glinted. Her torso appeared even longer than it already looked in her tunic—a formidable sight. For a moment, she looked like a sumo wrestler trying to heave her opponent over one shoulder in a classic suplex move.

"What the . . ."

But she couldn't get her opponent off balance. The other sumo wrestler was even more formidable.

"This . . . damn . . ."

If you think about it, this was a door that the previous tenant, Mr. Kawamura, must have used on a daily basis. And yet the realtor could neither heave it over her shoulder nor corkscrew it to the mat. For a moment I imagined Mr. Kawamura himself on the other side of the door, feet firmly planted, gripping the knob with all his might. Mr. Kawamura and the realtor: two sumo wrestlers locked in a furious grapple at the threshold of the kitchen. When one of them crouched low, trying to pull backward, the other would reciprocate by going even lower, both parties grunting and groaning on either side of the door.

"Jeez . . . Mr. Kawamura . . . must have . . ."

Little by little, the realtor's arms grew weary. She went from having both arms wrapped around her opponent's chest to releasing her grasp entirely. Her shoulders went slack and her hands drooped toward the floor. She shot me a glance over one shoulder, her necklace glinting beneath her hair. The odor of back sweat wafted out from her collar.

"Don't—" I stammered. "Don't worry about it . . . It's no big deal . . ."

But the realtor went right back to grappling with the back door. She was determined to show me the rest of the property, even if it meant planting her feet and trying that same old suplex move again.

I started to get a little critical. Why was she repeating the same move over and over instead of leveraging the weight of her opponent? Why didn't she try pulling the chair or sweeping a leg?

At that very moment, she let out a giant "Mmmmvabitch!!!" and gave the door a swift kick. The door, for its part, was so concentrated on the knob that it was caught off guard. The bottom buckled, the latch popped free, and the door swung open. Surprised, the realtor staggered backward. She'd won the round with a brilliant leg sweep. The door swayed on its hinges, finally tapped out.

The realtor drew a deep breath.

"Well—this . . . is . . . the . . . uh . . ."

She was too exhausted to finish the sentence. She just stood there panting, glaring at the door. Both wrestlers had left it all out on the mat.

Looking over at the door, I noticed that the lower part of its plywood surface was covered in dents and beginning to peel in places—the legacy of years worth of punts from shoes and boots and sandals, no doubt. Mr. Kawamura and the rest of his family probably had to sweep the leg every time they used this door. While the knob accrued a resistant layer of rust, a fatal weakness developed below its belt. Over the years, the Kawamura family must have learned to attack this Achilles heel, and now the realtor had identified the same vulnerability. And I, by proxy, was also privy to the secret.

For anyone who didn't know, however, the door remained a formidable opponent. In short, there was no need to lock it—it wasn't the sort of door that could be unlocked simply by unlocking it.

The day I moved in, I kicked the door open and left it that way while I went out to eat spaghetti. I figured that my mass of unsorted boxes would be too big of a hassle for anybody to steal. But once I'd unpacked and situated my stuff, I started to feel like I should start closing the door properly.

This meant that every time I wanted to enter or exit, I would have to sweep my opponent's leg and win a round. And that simply wasn't going to be sustainable. Just thinking about it was exhausting. Sure, my record might improve with each bout, but there would inevitably be days when the first leg sweep wouldn't quite do the trick, and I'd have to resort to a little combo move: feinting left and going right; making like I was trying a suplex only to sneak in a leg. Just thinking about it was exhausting. So I decided to replace the whole knob.

I give Memori a ring. The selfsame Memori who assisted me with my gutters.

"Hey man, I'm gonna go buy a doorknob—a brass one."

"Hello . . . ? Um, this is Memori speaking."

"I know who you are; I'm gonna go buy a doorknob—a brass one."

"Oh—hi, Teach. Why can't you just say 'Hi' and maybe state your name like a normal person . . . ?"

"Yeah, sure, anyway—I've been thinking. Buying a doorknob would be really radical. Am I right?"

"You're still doing radical stuff?"

"Yeah, man. There's something really wild about how doorknobs are completely . . . embedded in the bulk of a door. You wanna come?"

Memori shows up a half an hour later on his bike—a profound testament to the excess of time on his hands.

"A bicycle, eh? Not a bad idea—let's take bikes."

I pull a red bicycle out from the back of the foyer.

"Bikes, man . . ." I say, squeezing the handlebars.

"Let me guess: bikes are radical?"

Even Memori's brain seems to have a lot of time on its hands.

"Naw, man . . ." I cringe. "Never mind . . ."

"Where are we going?"

"That same hardware store where we got the gutters. It's the biggest one around."

Side by side, we pedal our bikes down the street. A neighborhood worth of houses rolls by. Every last hedge is tidily trimmed; all the doors are primly shut. It's a rather demure bit of suburb.

"Doorknobs come in quite a variety of flavors," says Memori, working his pedals.

"True, if you're talking about the kind you put on a front door. I'm buying one for the back door. Who the hell puts a doorknob on their front door anyway?"

"Bad people, I'm guessing . . . ?"

"Yeah, man. Sliding wooden doors are where it's at. A front door isn't a front door unless you can whip it to one side with a rattle. Turning a little knob and swinging the door open? That shit should be relegated to the back."

"Ah—I'm guessing your new place has a sliding door?"

"Well, duh. Who the hell would put a back door on the front of their house?"

"Well . . ."

"Well what?"

"Well, I guess only a total simpleton would . . . ?"

"Yeah, only a simpleton would do that kind of thing. A simpleton or a coward."

We cruise up to the hardware store. I want to buy pretty much everything I see. But this particular day is imbued with a sense of doorknob-bound destiny. From the store's extensive inventory, I select a knob labeled:

H/BK INTERIOR DOOR SET #3660 STAINLESS STEEL

It costs me twenty bucks. I'm a little upset that it's not made of brass, but the H/BK is the only one that will fit my door. It's just a back door, after all. I'm pretty sure the H/BK will suffice.

Memori and I ride home. Once there, our first order of business is to eat the sherbet we bought on the way back. Melon for me, strawberry for Memori. Memori keeps giving my melon the eyes, but I don't even glance at his strawberry. The only time I notice it is when I look up from my own cup, so I'm pretty confident that my melon flavor is the more delicious of the two. Still, we both end up finishing at the same time.

"Well, then . . ."

I drag out my toolbox and select a screwdriver. I've never replaced a doorknob before. Sure, I've tightened the odd loose screw, but I've never actually seen the inner workings of a knob, as tempted as I've been to unscrew one and peek inside. I think I've always been worried that I wouldn't be able to reassemble it. But today is the day that I take that fateful step. This is no longer a matter of curiosity—I have a genuine need to fix the door. I can confidently remove every last screw.

With the placid mien of an experienced handyman, I press my screwdriver into a screw and give it a turn. The head of the driver slips out. I pause, take a closer look, and realize that I'm holding a Phillips head screwdriver. The screw is a flathead. This doorknob must be the old-fashioned kind. Embarrassed, I root around in my toolbox and pull out the correct screwdriver. Mercifully, Memori is facing the other way. He's trying to scrub cooking oil off the door, a look of sheer disbelief on his face.

"Man, this is one greasy door."

"It's not just the door. The whole kitchen is sticky like that. Every surface feels like a roach trap."

"Damn. A wall-to-wall roach trap."

"Ha ha—a wall-to-wall roach trap indeed. I can't believe the last tenant actually lived like this. One wrong move and you're stuck in roach purgatory."

"They must have figured out how to get unstuck, though."

"They did what it took to survive."

"Survivalists, yeah . . ."

I remove the screws one by one. The latch gets a little looser with each twist of my screwdriver. I slide both knobs off and extract the shaft, then poke gently at the edges of the housing until the whole box-shaped mechanism tumbles from the door in a cascade of dirt and wood powder. The smell of rusty iron hits my nose. The heart of the door is now a gaping hole. It's completely defenseless.

"Damn," I murmur. "Radical . . ."

Memori stops washing the kitchen door, stretches for a moment, then takes a look.

"What's going on?" he says. "How's it coming?"

"Fine, fine—it's just . . . once you pull the knob out of a door, there's really nothing there."

"Well, what did you expect?"

"I don't know. I just . . ."

I'm not sure how to explain it, but the knobless door almost looks like a man being robbed at gunpoint, the barrel of a gun pressed to the center of his chest.

I take the shiny new H/BK out of its bag and stab it right through the door's ribs. It looks like a good fit, but when I give the door a test close, the bolt doesn't quite align with the latch. I'm going to need to unscrew the metal latch and chisel away at the doorjamb to get the bolt to fit. So I pick up my screwdriver and twist out two tiny screws: one above and another below. The metal plate falls away, exposing a hole filled with ancient detritus. Every time this door opened or closed, the bolt must have thrust in and out, grinding away at the latch and whisking in dust and metallic shavings. Meanwhile, the kitchen's ubiquitous grease was also creeping in. With tip of my screwdriver, I start scraping out the particulate history of my house. It tumbles out onto the kitchen floor.

As I'm scraping, I notice something black up in the corner of the jamb. I tilt my screwdriver upward to poke it out, and the black mass suddenly moves.

It's a bug. A tiny spider, about five millimeters wide.

"Whoa."

The spider scrambles this way and that in the jamb, then gives up and abandons ship, racing up the doorframe on diaphanous legs. I can tell it's pretty freaked out about having its home pried opened and probed with a screwdriver. I wonder where it will go.

"What was that 'whoa' for?" Memori asks.

"Oh, nothing."

"Nothing?"

"There was a spider . . . in the latch . . ."

"A spider?"

It must have been living here. It had made a home for itself in this tiny square hole. Even a little gap like this can serve as somebody's home. A spider house. Why would it choose to live here, of all places? Maybe this was the only room it could find. Maybe the only listing on the market was this eraser-sized indentation, in and out of which a thick metal bolt sliced like a gigantic pair of scissors every time anyone opened or closed the door. Imagine how this spider must have felt, a gigantic blade shearing through its home every day. A tiny studio apartment into which a massive guillotine periodically bursts, cutting a swath through the living room—that's the sort of place this spider called home.

"Freaky . . ."

"Huh?"

"This hole was, like, a spider house . . ."

"A spider house . . ."

The guillotine would have struck frequently and without warning. It might come in the middle of dinner, its blade grazing one cheek as it passed. This would have gone on for years, the spider amassing a vast collection of scars as it ducked and twisted around the blade. But as the spider mapped out the guillotine's path, it began to find a logic in the horror. Fear lost sway as it built a life for itself in the little crannies just outside of the blade's reach. If the guillotine came screaming by mid-meal, skimming the edge of a teacup, the spider wouldn't even pause its chewing. It slept well, even as the blade grazed its snoring nose.

And now all five millimeters of this stoic bug scamper off in a huff.

"Man," says Memori, peering into the eraser-sized hole, "the only kind of web you could build in a hole like that would be, like, the size of a nosehair."

"Freaky, right?" I say.

I still feel like I'm in the middle of a nightmare, though. A nightmare lurking just a millimeter outside the everyday.

"Yeah, freaky," says Memori. "But imagine being the bug who gets caught in a nosehair-sized spiderweb all the way at the back of a door latch?"

This takes me by surprise.

"You think the spider was really catching bugs back there?"

"Yeah."

I don't know what to say. So I take a chisel to the abandoned spider home and widen it a little. Then I slap a brand-new latch over the hole, affix it with a brand-new screw, and swing the door shut with my brand-new H/BK handle. It closes with a brand-new click, brisk and clean. There's a newness and precision to the sound. It sounds like the shutter on a brand-new camera. I want to hear it again.

Swish.

Click.

Swish.

Click.

I open and close the door several times. I guess I'll be able to hang up my sumo belt for now.

Eventually this latch, too, will rust shut, and I'll have to go back to sweeping the leg every time I want to leave. But for the foreseeable future it looks like the door is going to open the normal way. I toss my screwdriver into the toolbox and slam the lid.

"I'm kinda parched."

"Yeah, me too."

"Sherbet?"

"Yeah."

We clean up our mess, close the door with a click, and pedal into town for another sherbet.

MONTH E, DAY E (CLOUDY)

I feel like L-brackets might be pretty radical pieces of hardware, but I haven't made up my mind. Are they truly radical? They've got to be radical, right? I mean, we're talking about cast-iron shelf brackets, here. Twenty-eight of them to boot.

I slide open my closet door. Behind rows of cardboard boxes lies a lumpy paper bag. It's one of those large department store bags with twine handles that you get when you buy a coat or something. And it's lumpy. By which I mean: in some places it's all caved in, while in others it's been ripped open by the tips of the brackets.

Cast-iron L-brackets for bookshelves. Twenty-eight of them to boot. And while there's no real reason why you shouldn't be able to arrange them in a more orderly fashion, the truth is that there's no good way to arrange L-brackets in a bag so they stay lined up. Which is so frustratingly counterintuitive that I can't even stand to think about it. Why do bookshelf brackets have to be like this?

And then there's the process of affixing them to the wall. Each bracket requires three screws, which mean you need six screws per shelf. Except that it's impossible to get all six to go in straight.

First, you've got to locate your stud and make little marks on the wall where each screw is supposed to go, then you have to drill three holes, but by the time you get to the third hole something is always out of whack, so you try re-drilling in the correct place by poking your bit right through the bracket itself, where it promptly gets stuck, compelling you to force it a little, at which point the tip of your bit breaks off and now you're out a drill bit. Why are shelf brackets always like this? And I've got twenty-eight of them to boot. Twenty-eight of the damn things, just going to seed in the back of my closet. To be honest, it's all quite radical. Distinctly rad. Perhaps the most radical of all possible radicalities. In other words, I should probably call Mr. Memori to discuss it. So I do.

"Those iron brackets for bookshelves are really radical, right?" I venture.

". . ." says Memori.

"Like, genuinely radical."

". . ." says Memori.

"I'm talking the real McCoy here."

". . ." he continues.

"Hyper-deluxe radicality."

". . ."

Transcribed, Memori is just one continuous stream of ellipses. I can almost feel the beaded string of dots popping out from the receiver and dangling there. The ellipses keep coming and coming, like I'm pulling up a potato vine—a continuous string of potato punctuation. One good yank and a whole pile of spuds will come tumbling out of the receiver.

"Memori."

". . ."

"Hey, Memori."

". . . . ."

"Yoohoo, Mr. Meeeemori!"

". . . . ."

Only then do I realize that I forgot to dial. I picked up the receiver and started gabbing from the gun.

I place the receiver in its cradle. The room has gone quiet. Nobody is talking.

"Ahem. Ahum."

I clear my throat a couple of times, stand up, flip on the light. It pops, crackles, snaps to life. Something about the whole situation feels a little too sincere. I'm kind of embarrassed, to be honest. The fluorescent light is being needlessly serious. I gaze at it for a while, until I begin to suspect that this light, too, may have been radicalized. Poor humanity, I think.

I pick up the receiver again. This time I'm careful to dial.

"Hello. Hello. Hello. Hello. Hello."

"Um . . . Memori speaking . . . ?"

"So this is Memori, is it?"

"Oh, it's you, Teach."

"Yeah it's me—hey, tell me your thoughts on L-brackets."

"Huh? Brackets? Like square parentheses?"

"Not that kind of bracket—shelf brackets. The L-shaped ones. That hold up bookshelves, you know?"

"Oh. Are you being radical again?"

"Yeah. You feel me?"

"Sure," he says. "Shelf brackets are radical. Categorically radical."

"Aha! I knew it!"

"You are correct in your assumption."

"How do you know?"

"How do I know? Well . . . I guess they just feel radical to me. Those brackets that hold up bookshelves, right? It's hard to explain."

"I knew it. I just knew it!"

Memori has confirmed my suspicion. It would be weird enough for a hardware enthusiast to have twenty-eight shelf brackets lying around, much less a layperson like myself.

"How many L-brackets do you own, Memori?"

"Not a single one."

"What? Not even one?"

"Nope. Can't say that I own any brackets at all."

"Well, shit. There's nothing radical about *that* . . ."

"Hmm . . . Yeah . . . I guess not."

"But man, brackets can sure be crazy. They're these skinny little pieces of metal, but they're all L-shaped, and they're nearly impossible to arrange in a paper bag. They always end up poking through and sticking out all over the place."

"That's what happens with L-shaped stuff . . ."

"Damn right! Everything would be fine if they just stayed lined up, but that never happens—they always get all tangled up so you can't pull one out without ripping apart the whole bag . . ."

I hang up the phone. Just talking about it is pissing me off. Why do shelf brackets have to be like this?

It all started with a single pair. Two shelf brackets and one shelf. This was back in my first apartment. I think I used the shelf for plaster sculptures or something—I was still in school at the time. When I moved, I brought the brackets with me, taking care not to lose the screws. Then I promptly affixed them to the wall of my new apartment. A few moves later and those first two brackets had multiplied into eight. I'd accrued more shelves because I'd accrued more stuff, and with each subsequent move, new possessions kept materializing. I got rid of a lot of stuff during Operation Entebbe, but every time I turned around it seemed like more stuff had popped up where the old stuff had been. Then, last year, I found myself alone in yet another new home, fretting over the oppressive amount of stuff on my floor. I couldn't shake the feeling that it was all clinging to my feet. I wanted to take that entire oppressive mass and shelve it. I wanted my tatami mats to see the light of day.

Looking at the walls, I discovered that my house had come with four preinstalled shelves. These were already jam-packed, but I noticed that the area above them was still completely bare. As were the upper walls of the hallway. So, too, the upper walls of the kitchen. The upper walls of the bathroom were likewise vacant. With my eyes up near the ceiling, I began to feel empowered. I felt invigorated, ready for a fight. These were alpine peaks, and I meant to scale them.

Like a true alpinist, I began mapping out my climb. A shelf here, a shelf there—I tallied the number of shelves my walls would accomodate and calculated the number of brackets they would require. I arrived at the startling figure of twenty.

So I hastened to the hardware store, billfold in hand.

"I need some brackets for hanging bookshelves. The L-shaped kind."

The shopkeeper emerged from the back of the store. I repeated myself:

"I'm looking for some of those cast-iron bookshelf brackets—do you have any in stock?"

"Yup, sure do."

I had framed my question as a matter of "stock" because I wasn't sure if a tiny hardware store like this would have twenty shelf brackets on hand. If I bought out their entire inventory, I'd feel bad for everyone else in the neighborhood who was building shelves. But the shopkeeper sounded pretty confident.

"How many do you need?"

I mustered all the dignity I could.

"Twenty."

"That's an awful lot of shelving, son."

"Yup," I said as nonchalantly as possible, with a look that said: *No time to explain, buddy, but trust me; I'm an interior alpinist.*

The shopkeeper, for his part, didn't seem to care. He just silently untied the twine binding a stack of L-brackets and began clangorously counting them out.

The following day I set about putting up shelves. It goes without saying that I called Memori for help. He was hanging out with a girl from the art school, so the two of them rode over on their bikes. I can't remember the girl's name, but I do remember the first thing out of her mouth when she came through the door:

"Wow. Look at all this . . . stuff!"

"No joke," Memori had concurred, "You've got a lot of stuff."

This all took place in my previous home.

"No joke? What's not a joke?"

"I mean, you don't joke around with your stuff. It's like, you're really careful with everything you own . . ."

Somehow Memori had managed to say something entirely different from what he was actually thinking. What he was actually thinking was that most of my stuff was junk. But what could I do? I turned around and slid the closet doors open, pulling out my brand-new shelf brackets and wordlessly displaying them to Memori and his friend. Twenty of them, all brand new. I was practically bragging out loud: *Pretty cool, right?* Except that I didn't actually need to say anything because my facial expression already said it all.

"What are those?" blurted out the girl, whose name I've since forgotten.

"We're gonna put up shelves," I said.

"Ohhhh, those metal things underneath shelves! I've seen them before in old houses."

"Jesus," interjected Memori, "You sure didn't skimp on the brackets . . ."

"What are you gonna do with them all?" the girl asked.

"Build shelves," I said."I already bought the wood."

I pointed up at the wall and outlined my plan for ascending the mountain.

"No way!" said the girl. "Why would you want so many shelves?"

"To shelve stuff," I said.

"On the shelves?" asked the girl. For some reason, this was surprising to her.

"Well, yeah. That's why we're putting them up."

"But don't you think it'll feel a little . . . oppressive? With all that stuff hanging over your head?"

"Oppressive? I'll tell you what's oppressive: all this junk swamping my floor! There's a ton of free space up there on the walls. Moving everything up there seems like a nice, practical solution."

"I don't know about *practical* . . ." she said.

Memori had gone mum, content to let the girl dictate conversation. I got the sense that he didn't really care one way or another. He probably just thought it was dumb to have opinions about someone else's shelf-making. I turned to the girl.

"You're telling me you don't build shelves when you move somewhere new?"

"Of course not."

"Really?" I wasn't buying it. "Where do you put all the stuff you've accrued? Your old books and everything? You can't just leave it lying around on the floor—you gotta shelve that shit."

"I don't *accrue* stuff."

"Yeah, but . . . it's kind of inevitable, right? Stuff just sort of . . . accrues."

"When I don't need something, I generally just throw it away."

"Yeah but there are some things you can't just throw away . . ."

"Like what? Why would you keep something you don't need?"

I didn't have an appropriate reply to this, so the three of us went to the train station and drank a lot of beer instead. I talked about shelves the entire time. Apparently the walls of newer condominiums and public housing projects don't even have studs from which shelves can be hung. Which means there's a whole generation of kids who don't know the first thing about shelving. They probably don't understand the literal meaning of "shelving" a project. I bet they don't even pronounce the "v" in "shelving" anymore; if you were to ask them, they'd just say: "Shelling? Is that, like, when you put a bunch of shells on something? Like a shell necklace or shell earrings?" All of which seems problematic to me. What are they even teaching in Japanese classes these days?

I continued on in this vein, gabbing away about shelving and cracking bad puns. These bad puns made me think about shelf necklaces and shelf earrings: clunky L-brackets dangling from tiny golden chains, maybe even with wooden boards attached, all of it swinging from your neck or ears. Think about it: what if we took all the shit we've accumulated over the years—the debt and the alimony and the boxes upon boxes of needless junk that have to be hauled from place to place—and shelved it onto one gigantic piece of jewelry that could be worn around proudly . . . or wherever this metaphor was going.

I went home. Flipping on the lights, I gazed up at the alpine slopes of my walls. I'd had a little too much to drink and it felt like several shelves were hanging from my head. But I was still determined to get at least one shelf hung.

Taking two brackets from the bag, I tipsily aligned them with two studs, marking where the screws should go. Then I picked up my drill and began boring into the walls. Finally I began screwing in the first bracket. I was already on the second screw before I realized that I was putting up one of my original brackets—I'd taken it off the wall during Operation Entebbe. It had belonged to the shelf above my desk in that sticky superglue apartment. In retrospect, it was funny that I'd gone through the trouble of unscrewing this bracket and taking it with me, in the midst of all that drama. I must have unconsciously chosen it because I was worried it would go to waste if I didn't use it first. It was identical to the new ones in terms of form and function, but there was something distinct about its patina. It was a different shade of green. This wasn't so much a matter of pigmentation as a function of time. The bracket had bumped into things and rubbed up against surfaces; it had been smudged by substances and tickled by smoke and human breath. After all this exposure to living spaces, its surface felt like the hide of an old animal.

My mind had been wandering. When it returned to the task at hand, I found that I'd wasted several screws on a single hole. The hole wasn't properly aligned, and I'd been forcing it. It felt cruel, the way I'd stripped those screws. I stuck with it, though, and eventually I coaxed all twelve screws through their respective holes, six on the left and six on the right. After that, I had to stop and catch my breath. I just didn't have another shelf in me.

For the hell of it, I placed a paper bag on the brand-new shelf. I still had eleven unopened boxes and eight paper bags of stuff to shelve. Placing one bag on a single shelf wasn't even putting a dent in all that stuff.

Something pink peered out at me from the bag. It was round and pointed and had two eyes. A kewpie doll. A remnant. The woman from the canned food company must have forgotten to take it with her. This was all I had left of her.

I stood up, took the kewpie doll out of the bag, and sat it on the shelf. Then I sat myself down, too. Resting my chin on one hand, I gazed up at the lone shelf occupying an entire wall. I just didn't have another shelf in me.

All this happened at my last house. Ultimately, that would be the only shelf I ever hung. The rest of the brackets just languished in a bag, deep in my closet. Here in my new place, I haven't put up a single shelf. I can't shake the feeling that I'm being watched. I have this nagging sense that hanging shelves on the walls would violate some kind of law. And so all twenty-eight brackets sit stewing in the back of my new closet.

I stand up again and open the closet door. I have to drag five boxes out before I can get back to the darker depths where the cast-iron brackets lie in wait. They're splayed every which way in one of those giant paper bags they give you at the department store when you buy a coat. A tight mess of iron L's, all garbled together. Try to pull one out and the whole tangle will come out with it.

I call Memori. I still hadn't called him back after hanging up earlier.

"Hey, Memori?"

". . ."

He must still be upset with me for hanging up on him.

"Hey, sorry I hung up on you. The kettle was boiling over."

". . ."

Ah—that's right: I probably forgot to dial again. I have to say, I'm a bit shocked at my own performance tonight. Something's off. But as long as I'm talking to an empty line, I might as well finish.

"You know," I whisper, "shelf brackets are pretty radical after all."

I hang up the phone and leave it there, standing up to turn off the kitchen light. A single pull on the string and one fluorescent tube goes dark; a second tug and the other blinks off, leaving only the tiny glow of the power indicator.

to the touch

IT'S AN IMMACULATE DAY. Crisp and clear. The air is transparent, not a trace of impurity. Which feels ominous. As if something were about to happen—something untoward. It's making me anxious.

I think to myself: *This is a blonde bombshell of a day.*

I'm squatting on my porch. Looking out over my little yard. Four hundred fifty bucks a month. My landlord pruned the roses yesterday and left the trimmings all over the lawn. The leaves are already going limp, but the thorns still look primed to prick. There's something so vehement about the taper of a thorn—*I swear to god I'll gouge you, man!*—that you can't help but wonder whether it's ever really stabbed at all.

A wet flash flits across my field of vision. I hone in on its location just in time to catch another flicker. The first salamander of the year. Weaving through the thorns. Painting a path between blades of grass. Its whole body is brand new. Immaculate. An unused camera, fresh from the box. Not a single fingerprint on it. Wriggling through my yard.

Enjoy your tail while you've got it, sucker, I think. *Because at some point it's gonna get bitten off or stepped on, and then all you'll have is a nasty gash on your ass.*

The salamander flashes again, pushing through the bushes and into my landlord's yard.

Percussive sounds waft out from their house: the thud of something heavy, then a swish and a knock. When I first moved here I figured that this was the sound of someone doing piecework. This endless loop of *thud-swish-knock* has the telltale rhythm of manual labor. But there's never any strain or haste to it. It starts up as if on a whim, then disappears just as whimsically. And the noises always come from my landlord's house. A landlord by definition shouldn't need to do piecework to make rent, so my current theory is that his wife has taken up leatherwork as a hobby.

Another *thud-swish-knock* echoes through the air. The only other sound is that of the salamander painting its way between blades of grass. It's an immaculate day.

This kind of weather has always felt dangerous to me. Blonde bombshell dangerous. Cheeks as cheery and pale as a cloudless New Year's Day. Pupils so placidly glassy that you could drop a stone in and watch it sink all the way to the bottom. That's the kind of vacant, grinning beauty I mean: an empty head stuffed with silver blades. A whole mess of knives that at any moment could slice through these smiling cheeks and come flying out. Weather like this feels threatening. The very air wants to split open and unleash some unseen venom. An invisible mass of heat lightning gathers static in the distance. One tiny touch and—*ZAP!*—your whole body is broasted. Which is why living bodies need grounding. Everything is fine as long as the natural grounding between male and female is preserved. Men are grounded by metal. Metal is a man's friend. But a woman needs life-sized friends. Women lack any connection to metal. That's the problem. Without grounding, women collect static electricity. Static electricity that awaits a spark. A woman, swollen with electricity, awaiting a spark.

Oh man.

Still squatting, I swivel towards the house, the sunlight glistening off my hunched shoulders. A sparkling afterimage of the garden shrivels into my living room, where the television flickers noiselessly.

I turn my body back toward the yard, where a cabbage butterfly flutters fickly about, inspecting the foliage. It's bobbing between a fig leaf and a branch, then a flower, then back to the fig leaf, then the laundry line, a dress shirt, a branch, a hydrangea leaf. It looks like a powder puff applying furtive pats of foundation to the air, a coat of makeup that only increases the bombshell beauty of the day. The sky sinks slowly closer, leaning in until it looms over the yard. The air brims with transparency. I'm inside a glass house. Invisible blades close in from every direction. I can't move.

"Hey Dad, I'm home!"

It's my daughter, Walnut.

"Hey, honey."

"The sun came out after all!" she says. "The hydrangeas were still all wet when I left in the morning . . ."

"Did you leave your umbrella at school?"

"Oh no!"

"Oh no."

"Ha ha, settle down. I didn't take my umbrella today."

"You didn't?"

"No—it was already sunny by the time I left. But I had you there for a moment!"

"Ha."

Walnut tosses her bag onto the desk and grabs an ice tea from the fridge. A cool breeze wafts out from the kitchen and over to the porch. I take a deep breath. The butterfly is batting around the porch, flirting with the house again. I give it a glare and it flickers like a flame before bobbing back into the garden, off behind the laundry.

"A butterfly!" Walnut exclaims.

"It's been lurking."

"In the house?"

"Yeah, it keeps flying over to the TV and fluttering around in front of the screen."

"Maybe it's watching TV?"

"Ha, could be. Or maybe it thinks the TV is some kind of flower. Ah—speak of the devil. It's back."

The butterfly shoots across the porch and into the house, where it starts monkeying around in the glow of the TV screen.

"What a weird butterfly," Walnut says.

"It's acting like a cat . . ."

"A cat?"

"I think it's cleaning. It looks like it's trying to dust the TV with its wings."

"It's putting makeup on the screen."

"Exactly—makeup."

"Weird. I guess it's a girl butterfly."

And with that, Walnut switches off the TV. The screen sizzles, its glow evaporating like drops of water on a sauce pan. A grey lid closes over the pan and the TV sets about stewing, a simmering pot of static electricity. It presses into the tatami mat with the weight of a full-grown woman.

"Hey, whatcha writing?" Walnut asks.

"A bit about a barbershop."

"A 'bit' as in a story?"

"Yeah. It might turn into a story. But for now I'm still just free-writing."

"That's your job, right?"

"Yeah, kind of. I'm just supposed to write whatever I want."

"Weird job."

Walnut starts leafing through the manuscript on my desk.

"Don't mess up the order," I admonish.

"How come you're writing it all formal like this?"

Today I paid a visit to the barber. I regret doing this. I sometimes wonder whether the barbershop exists that one does not regret visiting.

I often find myself longing for a bygone era of haircuts. When I was a boy we all shaved our heads, which precluded any sort of regret. This was liberating. The strictly regulated scalps of Imperialism simplified things for the brains within. All a brain needed to do was sit quietly under its scalp. One entered the most proximate barbershop, submitted to a buzz, paid, and left. There was no need for a mirror, even. How simple! How carefree!

"'All a brain needed to do was sit quietly'? . . . You write weird, Dad."

"Heh, heh. But that's what it felt like. Back then, you couldn't think about your hair even if you wanted to. And there was a certain ease to that."

"Well, I'd be bored if I couldn't think about hair."

"But we weren't bored—we didn't know anything else was possible. And having your hair buzzed actually feels good."

"Then you should start shaving your head again."

"You're kidding, right?"

"But you said it feels good!"

"Yeah, I did. It does. A shaved head makes you feel like you've ditched unnecessary baggage. You literally feel lighter. But I guess it's something girls don't get to experience."

"Pssh. A girl with a shaved head . . . Wait—women who become Buddhist nuns shave their heads."

"Oh yeah . . . But they sure don't look any lighter for it. That's a heavy way to shave."

"Ugh—a heavy head." Walnut mulls this over. "But I know what you mean: bald heads look heavy."

"With Buddhist nuns, it doesn't look like they shaved their heads so much as their scalps started poking out from their hair."

"A bald head looks like it would sink in water. Like a cannonball."

"Kerplunk."

I amble over to the kitchen. Today seems like a good day for a stew, so I tumble a handful of potatoes into the sink. The knife I sharpened last night curls the skin right off them.

"Why don't I peel?" Walnut offers.

"Don't worry," I say. "I've got time."

"You don't really need to peel them yet."

"Sure they don't *need* peeling, but like I said: I've got time."

"Fine . . . But for real, Dad, I think you should just shave your head."

"Oh, I've gotten buzz cuts before. Twice, actually. After quitting school. But I regretted it both times. It made me depressed."

"Depressed? You?"

"I used to get depressed sometimes."

"I'd like to see you try to be depressed."

Walnut sits at my desk, flipping through my manuscript. She looks as though she's doing my work for me.

"And that's why you're so worried about barbershops?"

"Exactly. I've got this heavy jaw, so I look goofy when I shave everything off the top."

The shape of one's head is not as important as its contents; the cut of one's hair does not affect the nobility of what lies beneath. Of course I wholeheartedly agree with these sentiments—and yet I still find myself hemming and hawing in front of barbershops. I am forever glancing at mirrors. Every time I catch sight of my lengthening hair, my brain begins to hem and haw, expanding and contracting within my skull. I look in mirrors; therefore I worry about my hair. I worry about my hair; and thus I peer into mirrors.

In the good old days of Imperialism, nobody thought to peer into a mirror. The word "mirror" was simply a round, glassy signifier, the exact size of a shaved head. Or rather, the mirrors had moved onto our bald skulls. Our slick scalps acted as the mirrors. And thus the brains beneath them never really saw themselves.

But things have changed. The hair that slowly sprouted from our shiny scalps muted their reflectivity. Real mirrors began appearing in hallways, over dressers and desks, in all the nooks and crannies of our lives. They held our brains at eye-level, compelling us to fuss over the cut of our jibs. This is why the act of choosing a barbershop is so fraught. The head hems and haws in a hall of mirrors.

Things are easier if one already has a regular barbershop, of course. The problem arises when moving to a new neighborhood. Walking past the hairdressers of a new locale, the head brims with the question of which, if any, to enter. The head becomes so saturated with the question of its own cropping that it begins leaking through the scalp, pressing one's hair out further and further.

"Wow, heads really are a headache," says Walnut. "But what do you mean by a head being a mirror? That sounds super fragile."

"Fragile?"

"Yeah. You always say things weird on purpose."

"It's not on purpose . . . I was just trying to express this ideology of a bald head as a mirror. As a conceptual ideal."

"Ideology, ideology—I heard someone say that everyone had an ideology in the old days."

"People still have ideologies!"

"Yeah, but there were more of them back in your day, right?"

"We're not talking about potatoes, here."

"It's just weird. I get that ideologies exist, but I've still never seen one in real life."

"Oh man. Look how many potatoes I just peeled!"

Ten potatoes lie in the sink—way more than we need for two servings of stew. This is enough for six adults: three meals for each of us and then some. Walnut gets up and takes a look.

"Yikes, Dad! What are you going to do with all these potatoes?"

"I don't know. I hadn't planned on peeling so many. I guess I'll slice them up and fry them in butter?"

"Once they're peeled, you gotta use them. But then somebody's gotta eat them, too. Remind me again: who was it who said they had just enough time to peel potatoes?"

"Ha. You got me there."

"What were you planning on making? Stew?"

"Yeah. Tomato stew."

"Tomato stew. Okay. We'll need carrots, then. Let me do the peeling this time."

"No, no—you go back over there and read me the next part."

"Oh, so you've got just enough time to peel some carrots, too?"

"Exactly. Peeling always feels like a waste of time, but that's what I like about it."

The fridge slams shut and Walnut brings over the carrots and onions.

"Here you go."

"Thanks."

"Don't overdo it this time."

"Gotcha. I'm feeling confident about my prospects with the carrots."

Peeling carrots doesn't feel nearly as productive as peeling potatoes, because their skins are translucent. With potatoes, you get to shave away this earthy husk, exposing the crisp white flesh underneath. Plus you can roll them around in one hand as you go: peel, roll, peel, roll.

Out on the porch, the sun has begun to wane. Walnut goes back to my desk.

"Let's see . . . Where was I . . . ? Oh yeah, you were looking for a barbershop. 'The head becomes so saturated with the question of its own cropping that it begins leaking through the scalp, pressing one's hair out further and further' . . . Jeez, Dad, this is so formal! It sounds like an essay you'd write in school."

And so it went until yesterday.

This last summer I made an unanticipated move to Q City. I jammed all of my unanticipated boxes into my new closests, and stacked the remaining ones in the corners of my new rooms, until I felt organized enough to head out and reconnoiter the new neighborhood. In quick order, I located the bathhouse, the hardware store, the liquor shop, and so on—until all that remained was the barber.

Now, finding a barbershop can be politely neglected for a few days. Indeed, finding a barbershop may be disregarded for a few weeks without significant repercussions. But after a month or two, nothing feels more urgent than the matter of one's hair. It sprouts thick and long even as one's head brims with the crux of its own cropping.

The selection of a barber affords no room for error, for the consequences of a bad haircut persist for an entire month. It takes three days for hair to grow a mere millimeter; in the meantime all one can do is wait.

This is most regrettable. The high stakes involved in a haircut make it impossible to casually step in for a trim. Instead, one finds oneself scrutinizing the local hairdressers with disproportionate rigor, sizing up each candy-striped pole like a poor man about to spend their life savings on a house.

Picture this: a lonesome old barbershop, far-flung from the train station, complete with three antique barber chairs, mahogony-framed mirrors with peeling varnish, and a brass doorknob worn shiny by years of use. Now conjure up the bald barber: ensconced in an old chesterfield, the springs poking through its upholstery. He sits there, puffing a pipe as he peruses the oversized headlines of the sports page. We are all familiar with this cliché, a trope as well-worn as an old washbasin.

I like these barbershops. I enjoy the mood they evoke as I walk past them. Yet they possess far too powerful an aura for me to ever push through their doors, for I know what awaits me within: the sides of my head tapered up like a seashore, my hair parted at a precise 7/3 ratio and pomaded into a rigid sculpture.

And so I pretend to peer into the bakery across the street as I walk slowly past.

Put to paper, this may all sound a bit overwrought. But the eraser does not exist that can rub out a haircut. Every trip to the barber condemns one to a month of incarceration in the reality of one's hair.

My new neighborhood has just this sort of antiquated barbershop. It's right next to the train station. You step out of the turnstiles onto a busy shopping arcade and there it is: sandwiched between a crowded fishmonger and a bustling grocer, teetering on the edge of bankruptcy, as if the building it occupied was condemned and its tenants were merely squatting until demolition day. How did this anachronistic barber come to occupy such a prime piece of real estate? It feels unnatural. The only explanation I have is that the barbershop must have been here long before the station. Only after the railroad came through town did a succession of newfangled malls and arcades spring up, hedging the barbershop in so that now it looks like it would rather just go out of business than deal with its new surroundings.

My initial instinct was to avoid the place entirely. I knew that venturing inside would mean submitting to seashore sides. This is the horror of visiting an unknown barber. All I really want is a tame, easygoing trim.

This is not to say that I prefer going shaggy. Maintaining an aesthetically pleasing shag is every bit as onerous as keeping one's hair short.

One's hair, meanwhile, continues to grow unabated.

Of course there are barbershops that specialize in this shaggy look. My new neighborhood features just such an establishment. Unlike the old-fashioned barbershop next to the station, it sits in a back alley off the main drag. I'm not sure whether the choice of location was intentional, but this shag-forward barbershop has a freshly renovated interior, complete with posters of various hairstyles. It feels more like a brand-new stereo than an old washbasin. Customers can get permanents and treatments, much like at a beauty salon.

This sort of establishment scares me as well. I get the sense that they have some sort of agenda—like they're going to try and foist some newfangled style upon me. I just know that if I push through their doors, I will wind up with my hair fried, dyed, and laid to the side. Drop my guard for even an instant and my cheeks will be rouged with powder, my eyes lined with kohl, my lips coated in crimson lipstick even as I plead: "You've got me all wrong! This isn't what I wanted!"

Can you imagine? Well I certainly can, which is why I make a point of hurrying past this particular shop, mumbling about some imaginary business matter: "Goddamn Nakamura and his unrealistic delivery schedule . . ."

"Psh. You're not really worried that a barber is going put lipstick on you, are you?"

"No, of course not. But you could see it happening, right?"

"You make it sound like it actually happened to you, though. You're tricking the reader."

"But that's how those fancy hair salons make me feel."

"All you'd have to do is tell them to stop," Walnut insists. "Then again, maybe you *are* the kind of person who would just let a barber have his way with you."

"Right? Once I walk through the door, I'm all theirs. That's why it's so hard to work up the courage to go in."

"Hey—you're not overdoing the carrots, too, are you?"

"Don't worry. The carrots are just fine. The potatoes, on the other hand—what was I thinking?"

"You were probably thinking about something important."

"Nah, I was just spacing out."

"Let me peel."

"No, I've got it."

"Did you do the tomatoes?"

"Oh right. Let me boil them first."

I put a pot of water on the stove and drop in three big tomatoes.

I hate this part. Somehow boiling a tomato feels wrong. I have the same hangup about cooking cucumbers. The first time I encountered stir-fried cucumbers and celery at a Chinese restaurant, I felt like I was eating sashimi tempura—the experience exceeded my ability to imagine it. Then I made the same dish at home and the whole thing started to seem a little less weird.

Red tomatoes bob around in the boiling water. I cover the pot. Walnut is reading the rest of my story.

"Does your story just go on and on like this?"

At some point, however, one must choose a barbershop and push through its doors. And so one goes about like a man buying groceries or commuting to work, secretly shooting glances this way and that, appraising the neighborhood barbers. Behind a deadpan expression, one's eyes assess the polish of each newly purchased stereo, the bottom of every well-worn washbasin. Every candy stripe one encounters must be categorized as an upstanding establishment or a perfect disaster. The desire to hurry by collides with the temptation to stop and stare, the two forces canceling each other out so that, to an innocent bystander, one appears to be walking at a normal pace. But while one's legs may seem ordinary on the outside, their interiors are shot through with heavy iron rebar. It is an illusion of lightness, achieved by painstakingly lifting one leaden leg over the other. Like trying to pick up an egg with an industrial crane . . .

"What are you even talking about, here?"

"You don't know this feeling? It's kind of like, um—like when you're uncorking a bottle of wine, but you don't want to pull too hard because the cork will pop out and wine will spill everywhere, so you have to pull hard while pulling soft at the same time. That feeling."

"Okay, yeah. Like, um . . . when you put a lot of effort into not putting in too much effort."

"Exactly. When I was a kid, I had this job selling light bulbs where I had to lug around paper bags filled with dozens of bulbs. Light bulbs are super light, but you can't carry them lightly or they'll crack. So you have to sort of lug them around as if they actually weighed a ton."

"Like when you put water in the ice tray to make ice!"

"Yeah, yeah! It's a very specific kind of movement. Hey—you know what an 'insecurity' is, right?"

"Of course! I've got insecurities, too, Dad."

"They're not the sort of thing you want to brag about, Walnut."

"Yeah, but you were about to tell me all about yours, right? About how you've got so many insecurities?"

"No, I wasn't. I swear! Though honestly, I feel like people aren't nearly as insecure as they used to be. Nowadays everybody's got their dogs on leashes. But in my day you had to deal with random dogs lying around everywhere. Whenever you'd pass one—whew, it was nerve-racking . . ."

"You were insecure about that?"

"You bet I was."

"Whenever I see a stray dog, I just pretend I don't notice them and keep walking. If you start to run, they'll just chase you more."

"Yeah, but no matter how hard you try to walk normal, you can feel the dog staring at you, your legs unconsciously picking up speed . . ."

My body is intimately familiar with this manner of walking. It's something I used to do when walking past pharmacies. I remember the sensation of two opposing forces pushing and pulling at my body as I strode past pharmacy after pharmacy, desperately trying to maintain my abnormally normal gait.

This was back when I first became sexually active. In order to procure a certain rubber accessory, I had set out for my local drugstore only to find myself walking right past it. Sure, I was embarrassed, but I also knew that I could visit any of the innumerable other drugstores throughout the city. And so I changed course and headed for the pharmacy by the train station. This pharmacy was always buzzing with people, affording an element of anonymity. Amidst all that chaos, a condom could be procured and pocketed without attracting any attention. Add some mentholatum ointment to my purchase and the condom would practically disappear. Tack on some eye drops and antacids and there would hardly be any condom left to speak of. Throw in a toothbrush and maybe a thermometer—this was my train of thought as I strode right up to and past this second pharmacy.

I walked past the next one, as well, then the next one and the next, until I found myself quite a distance from the station.

Then I wandered back and forth along this same route until I had memorized the faces of the clerks at each pharmacy. Which of course meant that I couldn't go into any of them. So I got on a train and rode it for a while, gazing wistfully out at the rooftops of passing buildings before disembarking at last at some unfamiliar station. As the clerk in that far-flung pharmacy finished wrapping up my purchase, an age-old adage popped into my head: "What happens on the road, stays on the road."

Keep in mind that this was back before the convenience of vending-machine prophylactics. These days, the mental anguish I experienced in my youth has been expunged from our fair country—another reason why our minds are now at leisure, free to loaf around in our skulls.

The same goes for hair. Ever since the rise of shag, the taper has become noticeably scarce. And while a sharply defined coif isn't exactly an endangered species, it no longer predominates. Of course this doesn't mean that it's not still out there, lurking about. Compared to the shallow shoreline of a barbershop cut, the fjords and firths of contemporary shag must look like the work of an amateur to most barbers. I imagine them screaming in their heads: "A true coastline must maintain a straight taper out into the sea!"

This is the basic tenet of a barber's existence, after all, which is why my feet still dither at their doors. For who knows what lies behind the genial facade of each new barber? Who knows what powerful opinions will be unleashed upon my hair?

And thus I digress before the barbershops of my new neighborhood.

Walnut is silent.

"Well?" I ask.

". . ."

I pull the lid off the pot. The water is churning, the tomatoes swollen and red. I switch off the heat and fish out the tomatoes. After lining them up on the cutting board, I start stabbing at them with the tip of the knife, making little incisions in their skins.

"Ouch, hot!"

I pull at the slick skins with my bare fingertips and they come sliding right off, revealing the pink flesh beneath. Three naked, gelatinous balls remain on the cutting board.

"Is going into a barbershop really that hard for you?"

Walnut moves onto the patio and squats down to gaze at the garden.

"Not as hard as it used to be. Young people don't get their hair shaved up the sides anymore, so that helps. Barbers have gotten a little more nuanced about the sides."

The garden is still shamelessly bathing in sunlight. The laundry, dry on the line, is too bright to look directly at.

"I think I might get a haircut, too," Walnut declares.

"Yeah?"

"Long hair makes me look old."

"Nothing wrong with that."

"No middle-schooler wants to look old, Dad. Ah—a salamander!"

Walnut gets to her feet and scrutinizes the grass. Her hair hangs delicately down below her shoulders. There was a time when she liked to keep it braided; there was a a period where she always kept it in a bow . . .

"That same salamander was here earlier," I say.

"It's pretty. I just hope it doesn't get any closer—ew!"

Walnut comes running back inside.

"You gonna get a bob cut?" I ask.

"Yeah, I like my hair in a bob."

"You can get a bob at the barbershop."

"No way. Girls go to beauty salons, not barbershops."

"What do you mean? Little girls have gotten bobs at the barbershop since time immemorial."

"Little girls, Dad. I'm starting middle school—I'm a young lady."

"Pretty much an adult."

"Especially when my hair grows out . . ."

Walnut is looking at the tomatoes on the cutting board. With their skins off, they don't look embarrassed so much as in pain. Walnut turns away and walks out into the garden. She reaches up to feel the laundry while I arrange all the ingredients on the cutting board: skinless spuds, skinless carrots, skinless onion, skinless garlic. And the skinless tomatoes.

"Well then, I guess we'll have to go to the salon. It's gotta be expensive, though, right?"

"Everything's expensive these days."

"What'll it cost—like thirty bucks? I understand spending thirty bucks on something that you get to keep, but thirty bucks for a haircut?"

"There are cheaper places out there. My friend's sister—she

graduated high school, so she's actually a grown-up—she told me about this one salon that will cut your hair for nine dollars."

"Wow. That's cheaper than the barbershop. Even a barber will charge you twenty bucks."

"I told you, Dad—everything's expensive these days."

"Smartass. You got somewhere in mind you want to go to?"

"I'm still getting a feel for the new neighborhood, but there's that one place above the stationery shop . . ."

I turn on the burner. Pieces of pork start sizzling. They huddle toward the middle of the saucepan, popping off little spritzes of oil, tiny dogs agonizing under a blazing sun. I lose my appetite immediately. Why did I decide to make stew on such a hot day? The meat was totally unnecessary. But it's already seized control of the entire recipe, popping and hissing with the authority of pork.

"That's some noisy meat," remarks Walnut.

"Yeah. It reminds me of how life used to be."

"Life?"

"Yeah, life."

"By 'life' do you mean 'stew'?"

"Forget about it."

"I can't hear you over all the frying. Did you put the garlic in?"

"Yeah, that's the first thing I put in."

Next I throw in the peeled vegetables. The pork's authority is hushed, buried in plant matter.

"I think your old man might head to the barber, as well."

"You're pretty shaggy," says Walnut. "Let's go together."

"I don't know if I'll be able to go through with it, though. I guess the place I went last time wasn't so bad . . ."

"You're so self-conscious."

"I'm not self-conscious—I just look ridiculous with short hair. But I don't want long hair, either . . . You know?"

Walnut starts giggling about something.

"What?" I say.

"Why don't you come get your hair cut at the beauty salon with me?"

"No way! A beauty salon? I ain't trying to win no beauty prize, babe."

"Babe?"

"Ha ha—just kidding."

"Lots of guys get their hair cut at the beauty salon these days."

"No thanks."

"Don't worry, Dad, they're not gonna put lipstick on you."

"Cut it out."

"Whatever. If you're so worried about lipstick, why don't you go to that barbershop from your story—the old run-down one?"

It doesn't sound like such a bad idea: why not go to that well-worn washbasin of a barbershop? That washbasin with a hole in the bottom. Walnut and I used to speculate about it whenever we passed. You can tell it's a barbershop by the candy stripes, but there are always random boxes and luggage stacked out front. Peeling varnish and lopsided doors betray its age, but it's hard to infer much else about it. Over time I stopped noticing it altogether, and nowadays I walk by without giving it a second thought. It helps that the lights are usually off.

Every once in a while I'll see a customer inside getting a cut, and I'll think, *Oh yeah, that's a barbershop!* But then the next time I pass, they'll be holding a rummage sale out front and I'll forget all about the barber lurking in the wings. Still, something about this idle and bygone establishment fits in perfectly with the rustic tone of the neighborhood.

"You know what? I think I'll go to that barber from the story after all."

"Right? They might secretly give the best cuts in town. For half the price."

"I don't know if I'll be able to go through with it, but I guess it can't hurt to take a look."

"I'm going to try that place above the stationery shop."

I flip off the gas. The stew goes still in the saucepan.

Walnut and I leave the house together, locking the door behind us. The town around us arcs gently toward dusk. We part ways at the stationery shop.

"Whoever finishes first goes and waits for the other person, okay?"

A beauty salon is bound to take more time than a barbershop, so I slowly mosey out onto the main drag. The cries of the fishmonger and the green grocer are growing rowdier with the approach of dusk. From a distance, I can see a salesman sitting in front of the barbershop. It looks like he's selling sewing machines. A sense of relief floods over me at the realization that the shop is closed. I guess I'll have to try again some other time. For now, it looks like I'll be visiting a normal barber.

As I pass, however, I notice a single light bulb burning in the dim window.

"Excuse me," I say to the sewing machine salesman. "Is the barbershop open?"

"Oh, sure," the man replies. "They're open. Open for business."

I pause, teetering on the brink. But I've already enquired—I can't just walk away. Putting on a skeptical expression, I push through the old glass door.

Right as I enter, a man in a white frock comes bursting out of the back, clutching a steaming cup of milk. He's wearing green and yellow track pants and wooden Japanese sandals under his barber's frock. The outfit strikes me as strangely incongruous. The man—ostensibly the barber—strides right past me without a word.

"May not be as hot as you like it," he says, handing the milk to the sewing machine salesman. "Sorry about that."

"Thanks," says the salesman. "You really didn't have to."

There's something odd about all this. The owner of the barbershop is displaying deference toward a salesman occupying the space in front of his shop. And while drinking hot milk on a warm midsummer day isn't completely unheard of, something about the opaline color of the liquid evokes the blonde of a bombshell.

Without so much as acknowledging my presence, the barber rushes back to the rear of the shop, where he starts fumbling around with a stack of towels.

"Are you open?" I call out after him.

"Yup, you bet. Let's getcha started."

He says this with what could be construed as the nonchalance of a craftsman. I take another look around the shop. On the floor: a rubber ball and a plastic toy train. On the walls: three large mirrors, the mercury peeling at the edges. Also featured: those elaborately upholstered chairs unique to barbershops, piled high with knickknacks and household objects. The barber clears them away before gesturing for me to sit.

"Yup . . . there we are . . . let's getcha going."

It looks like this is actually happening. I hang my tote bag on the wall and sit down. The barber immediately begins spritzing my scalp with water.

I have no choice but to stare at the mirror in front of me. As my hair grows wet and flaccid, my excess of jaw juts into view. Honestly, I can't stand the shape of my face. I want to look away, but my purview is pure mirror. I hate being in front of mirrors.

The barber begins brushing my hair out with the fingers of both hands. There's a certain rhythm to this—the rhythm of barbershops.

"Scuuuse me, there."

He reaches around from behind, unbuttons the top of my shirt, and folds back my collar. Then he begins wrapping my neck in a towel. Most barbers wrap you in a towel right away, but this guy makes sure that my shirt is all the way open, my neck fully exposed. He keeps pulling at my collar, as if it won't fold back far enough.

“Scuuuse me. You mind if I open you up another button?”

The barber unfastens another button. I always leave my collar open, so at this point we’re already three buttons down, my shirt open halfway to my shoulders. I don’t understand why he needs to expose so much skin.

“Scuuuse me.”

He continues wrapping my neck. His voice is gentle, affecting a carefree drawl, but his hands work with brute force. He jams a towel down into my shirt, giving it one last shove just for the hell of it. This last thrust is completely unnecessary. There’s something disconcerting about this. I understand that this is a barbershop, but I can’t help but feel like I’m about to be butchered. A twinge of regret shivers through me.

The barber runs his fingers through my hair, then throws a white apron over me. He begins inspecting my face, taking inventory of my pimples:

“Here . . . And here . . . and then here.”

Suddenly, he notices my nose hairs and takes out a tiny pair of scissors. Some barbers will trim your nostrils, but this is usually done after the haircut. A look of suspicion flits across my face. The barber is quick to pick up on this.

“Dontcha worry. Just sit back and relax . . .”

Assuming the tone of a doctor, he inserts his scissors into my nostrils, giving each a few snips. It’s like having dessert before dinner.

After putting the scissors away, he resumes running his fingers through my hair.

"Now, then. How'd you like it done?"

"Relatively short, I guess . . . ?"

"Relatively short. All righty. You really let it grow out around the ears there."

"You don't have to part it or anything. I always just kind of let it hang down from the middle."

"I see—the natural look. That's certainly one way to do it. Okay. Must be a hassle, though . . ."

I have no idea what he means by "a hassle." The barber disappears into the back. I can hear him clanging around, preparing his scissors and other gear. I look at my face in the mirror. My face stares back with the tense expression of a petty thief in a mugshot. The situation is already out of my hands.

From up on a shelf, a transistor radio broadcasts the sumo tournament. I can hear the rattling of objects, the *ssszzikk* of metal being whetted. Then the barber reappears in the mirror, a comb in his left hand and scissors in his right. These scissors are abnormally large, bulging at the tips like a pair of French knives. For a moment I openly balk. But the barber doesn't pay me the least bit of mind.

"Alrighty," he announces, straightening himself up in the mirror. "Let's get started."

He begins snipping away with incredible speed. Five-centimeter locks of hair come tumbling down the sides of my head.

"Um—not too short on the sides, okay . . . ?" I say, but it's already too late. There's a Jonestown massacre of hair piling up on my apron. In recent years, barbershops have stopped tapering the sides unless you explicitly ask them to, and I had assumed that this would be the case here, too. I let my guard down.

"Mmkay. 'Not too short.' You mean, long enough to grab with your fingers like so?"

"I mean not very short."

My face in the mirror is visibly wincing.

"Mmkay. So the sides, for example, you want them long enough to sort of grab, like this, with your fingers . . . ?"

He puts down his scissors and stares at the remaining hair on the sides of my head, then begins tugging at it with both hands. Bringing his face in close, he cocks his head to one side and gazes at my scalp, deep in thought. It's as if his fingers were grasping something other than hair—a rare stamp, say, or a returned garment. He leaves the world of hair for a moment and fixates on something else entirely.

By now, I've resigned myself to my fate. Any attempt to reason with this man will be futile. All I can do is add new wrinkles of severity to my brow. Who knows what the rest of this haircut will entail. He's only just begun.

The barber switches to an ordinary pair of scissors and begins trimming away at my bangs and around the ears.

"Scuuuse me there. So, how do you wear your bangs?"

"I guess I'd like them evened out a bit."

He grabs my bangs and lifts them into the air, snipping three millimeters from a few strands before lifting up another segment and skimming off another two millimeters. He's barely cutting any hair at all now; whatever he's doing isn't even making a dent in my shag. I want to tell him to take off a little more, but I'm worried that he'll bring out the French knives again, so I bite my tongue, my brow frozen in multiple furrows. I can't begin to imagine what the shave will involve. The shave! Should I really let this man wield a razor around my face? Leaning back and offering your Adam's apple to a razor is already hard enough at a regular barbershop.

I begin frantically looking for a way out. While the barber futzes with my hair, I sneak a glance around the room, and notice what appears to be blood splattered on the tawny walls and the edges of the wooden shelves. What carnage has this room borne witness to? The first slip of his hand may have been an accident. But after mistakenly slicing off an ear or a nose, the barber probably felt that he could get away with carving off a bit of jowl or a buttock while he was at it. And then he was all-in, hacking his customer into little bits and stuffing them into a garbage bag in the back room . . . It's still light outside. Crowds of people are passing by as the salesman continues to hawk his sewing machines. Of course, it's entirely possibly that the salesman is in cahoots with the barber. Maybe he's there as a lookout to make sure nobody sees the horrors unfolding inside. As a frequent passerby myself, I've never really paid attention to the goings-on within this particular establishment. I may have registered on some precognitive level that people were getting their hair cut, but now I wonder whether those customers ever made it out alive.

The barber finishes his comb-and-scissor work and brings out the lather bowl. It's just as I'd feared: he intends to use a straight razor.

"Scuuuse me."

He sets about smearing shaving cream onto my sideburns. Again, the roughness of his hands contrasts with the gentle lull of his voice. He flourishes the foam in fat Fauvist strokes, spreading it all the way down my neck.

The sumo wrestling broadcasters are still chattering away on the transistor. I can feel myself getting irritated at the barber for taking his sweet time while I'm in this compromised state. Now he's off choosing a blade. Below a mirror at the back of the shop, a dozen or so knives are arrayed on a white tablecloth. They're all Japanese steel, but like the French scissors, none are blades I'm familiar with. He doesn't have any of the folding razors you typically see in barbershops. Instead, they're all short, fixed-blade deals, their handles wrapped in cheap blue rubber. They look like practice knives.

"Scuuuse me."

Before I know it, he's standing behind me. He takes a blade between his fingers and presses it to the back of my neck like a cattle brand. I clench my fists. Even if he strikes with all his strength, a cut to the back of the neck probably won't be fatal. My first concern will be blood loss. Survival hinges on how quickly I can react. Of greatest concern: the front of my neck and my Adam's apple, splayed bare beneath my chin.

His blade moves down my neck and into the regions exposed by my wide-open collar. He seems prepared to shave even the finest of hairs all the way down my back. After each passage over the slope of my neck, he returns to check for stray strands, grazing away any lingering baby hairs with the belly of his blade. He should be done by now, but he seems to be savoring the work. He takes a step back to evaluate from a distance, then comes in close for further perusal, a fisherman sipping whiskey while mending his pole. My neck is a thick fishing pole. It juts from my body, shiny and smooth.

At some point the barber finishes mending his pole and stands before me grinning. He's getting ready to shave my face. He stands erect, arms at his sides, back straight, gazing down at me. The way he looks at my face—it's as though he were staring at an inanimate object.

He situates the lather bowl and blade in front of the mirror, pulls the headrest up, and places a hand on the lever. At this point, it would probably be more dangerous to try to stop him. This is in god's hands now. I give my legs a stretch, refold my arms, and take a deep breath. The barber waits for me to complete my subtle readjustments before saying:

"You all ready there? Scuuuse me."

There's nothing to be "all ready" for, but I can tell by his tone that he sees right through me. He's timed his utterance so that it aligns precisely with my mental preparations. Were his other customers "all ready" as well?

"Here goes the chair now. Just leeean back."

Shaving cream is slopped onto my face with a callousness inversely proportional to the lilt of his voice. He applies coat after coat of foam until it seems as though the real goal at hand is the application of shaving cream. Lather billows up on my cheeks. While I can't actually see the mirror from my supine position, I probably look like one of Rouault's Christ paintings.

The barber disappears into the back of the shop, leaving me in a vulnerable state once more. I can hear him preparing a towel and pouring hot water. He's humming a cheerful ditty.

"Hummmmm, dee-dum-dee, dummmmm . . ."

His tenor is surprisingly high-pitched—the tune is from *Madame Butterfly*.

"Ooooone fine dayyyyy . . ."

A sensation of dizziness wells up inside my head. The barber's mismatched complexion, the incongruence of all of his bluntness and delicacy—it's all been scooped up and strung from the ceiling where it slowly spins, suspended by the silk thread of his tenor. I can't move. My body is bound flat to the reclined barber's chair like a piece of lumber.

Something else emerges from the rear of the shop. It appears to be a child. I can't see them, but I can feel them passing by the back of my head. The barber's tenor cuts out for a moment.

"Hey—watch your posture."

"Yeah, yeah," the apparition mumbles as it continues out the front door and onto the street. This momentary interjection of normalcy begins to melt away as soon as the barber starts humming again, his voice a silk thread stretching thinner and thinner until it's barely just a strand of cotton candy. The announcer on the radio suddenly grows excited.

They're locked, they're pushing, they're pushing, pushing!

"Hehehe . . ." the barber chuckles to himself. He's put on a white surgical mask.

I wonder whether I should try to talk to him about sumo, or if I'm better off leaving him alone. I worry that if I don't say something to break the silence, he'll only fall deeper and deeper into the spell of the razor's sheen, his eyes growing glazed and vacant. Then again, bringing up the sumo match might break his concentration, causing him to wield his blade all the more brusquely.

In the end, I give in to the need to speak:

"Which round of the sumo tournament are we on again?"

"Eh? Um . . . Let's see . . . the tenth day? Wait—the eighth? Hehe . . ."

"Ah—it's the third day."

"Is that right? Hehe. It's just not the same over the radio. I do enjoy watching on television, but I'm of the persuasion that if you're gonna watch some sumo, you oughta plop yourself down in front of one of them big wood cabinet televisions and really watch it—know what I mean?"

"Um, sure. Yeah . . . ?"

"Tell you the truth, I prefer me a sports with more muscular, toned bodies. I'd rather watch a rock-hard athlete—one with some nicely cut muscle on 'em."

Oh man. It's happening. I just didn't think it would happen so fast.

"I'll take boxing or bicycle racing over sumo any day of the week," he continues. "The muscles on them cyclists—whew! I can't get enough of 'em. I could just look at their muscles all day."

I'm thrown off by how unabashed he is about saying all this. He's almost being too straightforward for this to sound like a fetish. It's as if the man simply enjoys a good set of muscles.

For this tournament . . . should suffice . . . gonna need to . . . his belt . . . The announcer's voice is building toward a crescendo.

"Hehehe . . ." the barber chuckles.

As far as I can tell, these chuckles are directed at the radio broadcast. I interpret them as an expression of disdain for the wrestlers' soft, flabby bodies.

"Back in the day, when Rikidōzan and Jesse Ortega were wrestling . . . that was fun to watch . . . but nowadays they've even got women . . ."

He's pulling the blade over my throat, and it takes every ounce of my strength to muster a reply:

"You mean . . . women's pro wrestling?"

"And women," he continues, "they just can't put on muscle like a man can, no matter what they do. Their bodies just don't work the same, no siree."

He doesn't seem to care about anything but muscles. Meanwhile, his hands and his eyes are completely engrossed in my neck. He's already gone through three cycles of lather, shave, lather, shave, lather, shave. There can't possibly be any hairs left for him to barber. And yet barber he does, easing his blade over the curve of my Adam's apple like a fine-tipped paint brush.

"Hey, Dad."

Walnut's voice. Her haircut must have finished before mine.

"You're still at it, Dad?"

And that's it—I'm saved. Thanks to the presence of this third person, this menacing figure can return to being an ordinary barber.

"You look totally different," Walnut says.

"Hello there, little miss," says the barber. "What a lovely young lady."

The barber bends over, razor still in hand, and looks Walnut in the eyes. He doesn't seem the least bit surprised by the sudden appearance of this child. He straightens back up and moves on to my ears. Some barbers will shave the downy hairs around the edges of your ears, but this guy works his razor all the way up into my earholes, probing the inner walls. My head reflexively pulls away, my ear along with it. But the barber's blade dances cheek-to-cheek with me, following my ear's lead in a tango.

"Just hold on . . . There's still a bit of hair over here . . ."

Of course there is. My flight instinct is on red alert, but the end is already in sight. I can see Walnut out of the corner of my eye. She's wearing her brand-new bob. If the beauty salon had taken even a few minutes longer, I bet this barber would have wormed his way all the way down to my pubes.

At long last, he sets the razor down and pulls off my apron. I get out of the chair and begin moving toward the door, a smile of disbelief frozen on my face. I'm still on pins and needles as to how all this will end. What if the haircut is inordinately cheap? What if he only charges five or six bucks, and his razor continues to haunt me like the collateral on an unpaid debt?

"Let's see . . . That'll be seventeen dollars, please."

He's almost apologetic about the price, but it comes as a relief to me. It feels like a divorce settlement.

I slowly push my frozen body through the barbershop door and out onto the street.

"Wait up, Dad!" Walnut gets her sneaker caught in the door behind me.

"Dad!" She catches up with me. "This about your insecurities, isn't it?"

". . ."

"Say something, Dad."

"I . . . I just . . ."

"It's not that bad."

"Not that bad . . . ?"

The neighborhood teems with the smells of anonymous dinners. My head brims with the image of those naked, gelatinous tomatoes. Walnut tags along after me, gabbing about this and that.

We get home to find the evening paper jammed into the mail slot. Walnut opens the door, and we're greeted by the faint aroma of stew. Exhausted, I head to the kitchen and pull the lid off the saucepan. Tomato stew sits inside, still as can be. I flip on the gas.

symmetric

"GOCHISŌ-SAMA," SAYS WALNUT, setting her chopsticks on the table. *Click*—the chopsticks snap into a horizontal line next to her teacup. The finishing touch. The line you dash under the tally on a receipt.

I imagine Walnut is thinking the same thing, but then she says something completely oblique:

"I wonder what they say in other countries."

"Huh?"

"Other countries. When they're done eating—I wonder what they say."

"You got me. Your pops don't speak no English."

"They must say something. Something kinda like 'gochisō-sama.'"

If they do, I wouldn't know. So I scoop a little more rice into my bowl. All we've got left are some boiled vegetables, a little grilled smelt, and a couple of pickles. Not even enough to wrap up and put in the fridge. It's easier to just eat it, at this point. Oh, poverty.

This is how my mother must have felt. And now I'm feeling how she felt. How it feels to wear a starched apron. Housewife feelings.

"They gotta have something like 'gochisō-sama.'"

Walnut continues to ponder, gazing at the red apple we've set aside for desert and rubbing the blade of the fruit knife with the heel of her finger.

"Hey—stop that!"

"Eek! You scared me."

"You were spacing out. You're gonna cut yourself."

"Oh. Whoops! What was I spacing out about?"

"About 'gochisō-sama.'"

"Oh yeah. So weird."

"What's so weird?"

"Just, like, the way you can think about three or four things all at once."

"There's no way you've got that many things going on in that little head of yours."

"Maybe not. But sometimes it feels that way."

"You'd be done with your homework at lot faster if you could think about math and social studies and reading and home economics at once."

"Yeah, sure—but that's not what I mean. You can't really think about different things at the same time. Your thoughts just kind of get mixed up in your head sometimes, you know?"

"What's all this stuff on your mind?"

"I don't know, but it feels like a lot. You know what I mean, right? When different thoughts overlap in your head?"

"I bet you were thinking about the food you just ate, and the apple we're gonna have for dessert."

"Maybe, I guess. But maybe not. I feel like I was thinking about a bunch of other stuff, too."

"Well I was thinking about the food still left on the table, and about your grandma, and about housewives."

"Housewives?"

"Yep—housewives. How it feels to be a housewife. Your pops is a housewife, after all."

"Psh."

"What? I am! I'm a housewife."

"You don't even have boobies."

"No, I don't. And it'd be kind of weird if I did. Ah—but I do have the tips. Just the booby tips. Two of them, right here where they should be."

"Gross. You're being weird."

Yeah. I guess this is a little weird. I probably shouldn't pursue this train of thought any further. I have a talent for sussing out the most indelicate take on a subject.

So I scold myself. And as I'm scolding myself, I grab a grilled smelt by the tail with my chopsticks and convey it to my mouth. All that's left on the table now are some boiled vegetables and a couple of pickles. We're rounding the final corner on dinner. Oh, poverty. Housewife feelings.

Walnut is pondering something again. She's staring at the apple, rubbing the knife with her finger.

"Stop that!"

"Eek!"

"You're in sixth grade now! You can't just space out like that."

"Yikes, you're right. Thinking about stuff is dangerous . . ."

"Thinking about stuff is fine and dandy, but why don't you fold your hands in your lap while you think instead of playing with knives."

"Hehe."

"What's so funny?"

"I was just thinking about boobies. How come boys only have the tips?"

She's right. There's something confusing about this. It's a mystery. It doesn't make sense, no matter how you slice it. What is the point of these nipples we men wear around on our chests? I spent some time thinking about this years ago and couldn't figure it out back then, either. Ah, the male nipple: serving no function whatsoever, but tenaciously clinging to our chests like little shrunken appendixes.

I chew the tail of my smelt and continue to ruminate on the male nipple. This smelt here is your typical pregnant smelt—i.e. filled with roe. Hold on. Sorry to digress, but why are all the smelt at the supermarket pregnant? Exclusively female, in other words. What happens to all the male smelt? Did they just decide to skip out on the whole supermarket experience? Are they off gliding around in some distant ocean?

"You want part of this apple, Dad?"

"Sure."

Oh yeah—male nipples. I have no idea what these nipples are doing on my chest. Both sexes used to have tails, for example, but those disappeared. I assume we just didn't need them anymore. We didn't need our appendixes, either, and those likewise devolved. Our fangs have regressed, too. The thick hair that once covered our bodies has almost entirely receded. I've think I read somewhere that we used to have webs of flesh between our fingers for swimming, but those shriveled up and disappeared once we started living on land.

Then you have the male nipple. Nipples on men fell out of use a very long time ago, yet here they are, still hanging on for dear life. I imagine that men, too, must have once had full, ample breasts. We may have even breastfed our own children. But that would have been in the distant past, down near the roots of the evolutionary tree, back when mammals were still sorting out male and female roles. Somewhere along the line, the Mammalia class assigned the task of nursing sucklings to females and evolution took over from there. This means that the male nipple must have fallen into disuse long before our tails or appendixes did—back before the mice that preceded the rabbits that preceded the raccoons that preceded the monkeys that preceded us. Male nipples have been useless for eons. But as we've evolved, ruthlessly discarding or redesigning all the obselete parts of our bodies, these ridiculous male nipples have somehow stayed stuck to our chests.

This isn't just a human problem. Male lions and tigers have nipples on their chests. Ditto cows and dogs. I can't help but wonder how these other male mammals feel about their own pointlessly protruding paps. Are they weirded out by them? I sure am. They have no reason to be here. Or maybe they've been hanging around all these years in case of an emergency. Like that pile of rubber bands you keep in the corner of your kitchen cabinet because you might need them someday, even though they're so old and desiccated by now that they'd probably just fall apart.

"What are you thinking about, Dad?"

"Oh, I was just thinking about rubber bands."

"Rubber bands? You had an awfully serious look on your face for someone thinking about rubber bands."

My mouth must have slowed to a halt, because I can feel a mass of half-chewed rice and smelt huddled up around my molars. It's like spackle at this point. I set my jaw back in motion, masticating and swallowing as I speak:

"You know how at the supermarket they snap rubber bands around your eggs and stuff? And how I always end up tossing those rubber bands into that empty can in the pantry because it would feel like such a waste to throw them away?"

"Yeah, I put rubber bands in there, too. The ones down on the bottom are, like, glued to the can."

"Right? And the ones on the edges are so old and dry that they'd probably just crack and snap if you tried to stretch them."

"Seems kind of pointless to keep saving them."

"Exactly. You're absolutely right. But I still can't bring myself to throw them away. I get home from the supermarket with brand new rubber bands and something inside me won't let me toss them."

"Yeah, I get it. I'm the same way. But you should see my friend's mom. She doesn't just save rubber bands: she keeps all the clear plastic cartons from grapes and stuff. You know those crinkly fruit cartons? She's got them stacked up a meter high in a corner of the kitchen."

"Wow."

"And there are multiple stacks."

"Sheesh."

"It's bananas. The first time I went over to her house to play, I couldn't believe it."

"I bet."

"And it wasn't just the kitchen. The whole hallway was lined with stacks of ice cream cartons and yogurt cups, all organized by size and shape. Oh—and the craziest thing was the paper! You know those magazine inserts with blank backs?"

"Oh yeah, those."

"She has a stack of them in the pantry that reaches clear to the ceiling. My friend said there's even more in the closet."

"That's intense."

"I guess she's planning on using it to make notepads someday."

"Except that we all know that nobody has that much stuff to take notes about."

"I wonder what's gonna happen to all that paper . . ."

"It'll probably just sit there, quietly filling up pantries and closets."

My mouth is almost empty now. I've finished the smelt and their tails. I give the last scraps of vegetable a look-over. All I have to do is get these greens into my mouth and polish off the pickles and we'll be done.

"You know, your pops is kind of cheap in the same way. Everybody who grew up in the olden days is like that. It becomes a part of you."

"Yeah, but you know we're never going to use all those rubber bands, right? There's no point in keeping them around."

"You're right . . . I guess the nipples on boys are a lot like those dried-up rubber bands."

"Hey, that was sneaky. You're trying to talk about boobies again."

"I wasn't trying to be sneaky! Women have boobies, right? So men have a little bit of boobie, too. Have you learned the word 'symmetry' yet?"

"Nope."

"Let's see . . . So, um—so you know how when we eat mackerel, the left fillet and the right fillet are identical?"

"Yeah, but one side gets the bones."

"Sure. But imagine if you were to make a perfect incision, right down the middle of the fish, so that it was perfectly filleted: half the bones on the left and half on the right."

"Okay, yeah. So kind of like a mirror image."

"Exactly. That's what symmetry means."

"Oh, okay."

"The same goes for our bodies, too. If you bring your left arm and right arm together, they match up, right?"

"Yeah. Your left and right knees match up when you close your legs, too."

"Same for your left eye and right eye."

"Eww. I don't even want to think about eyes touching."

"Yeah, but we're being theoretical here."

This whole pattern of symmetry presents another mystery. The left and right sides of our faces are carbon copies of each other. We probably only need one side, but we always get two. Birds have identical wings on the left and the right. Spiders have the same number of legs on either side. It's always the same configuration, flipped over backwards. The north and south poles of the Earth are inverted copies of one another. Same for plus and minus. Savings and loans. Black and white. Day and night. Memory and forgetting. The day you're born and the day you die.

"Sunrise and sunset are a symmetry, too, right?"

"Exactly! Which is why there's actually a lunchtime in the middle of the night."

"There is?"

"Yep. Back in college I had this part-time gig as a shop dresser, decorating the displays in department stores. This meant I had to work night shifts. We would show up in the evening, right as the mall was closing, and work until the sun came up the next day.

We'd be working all by ourselves in these big, empty department stores, and when the clock hit midnight, someone would shout: 'Lunchtime, folks!'"

"Whoa—symmetry. Night lunch!"

"Kind of beautiful, right? I mean, lunch options are generally pretty limited come midnight, but it was still kind of nice."

"Night lunch sounds like a crater or something. But day lunch sticks out like a lump."

"Yeah, they're like the inside out of each other."

"Cool."

"Yeah, it's genuinely cool. But symmetry is a mystery, you know? Pretty much everything is symmetric."

"How come?"

"That's the mystery. Except I kind of feel like I know why."

"How's that?"

"Well, let's see. For example, men and women are symmetric."

"Oh . . . Yeah . . . I guess so."

That's right. Men and women. We have a symmetrical relationship. In terms of our bodies, we're generally more identical than symmetrical. But there are parts of us—namely the genitals—that aren't identical, though they maintain a sort of reciprocal symmetry. Over the long arc of history, our bodies have responded to the harsh demands of nature with a series of equal but opposite transformations—an image and its reflection in a mirror. The penis and the clitoris both share a general location, but one has expanded while the other has contracted. The gonads that bulge from a male's body conversely retreated up into the female form, where they dangle from the uterus. I have a memory from childhood of squatting over an old-fashioned toilet, staring down at my testicles in boredom, and being shocked to find them moving and churning about of their own accord, independent of my will. They dangled from my crotch like fishing lures, listlessly lilting up and down before rolling abruptly to one side. It was the first time I'd noticed a part of my body that existed beyond me—outside of my ability to control it. That gentle churning action somehow felt like it exceeded me. You often hear people wax poetic about how the uterus is its own universe, but I feel like I discovered something similar in my own body. I was one tiny part of the universe, but I could also fit the whole of the cosmos inside my body, where it formed another universe entirely.

"Dad."

"Yeah?"

"The apple's all peeled. You were spacing out. Thinking about something deep again?"

"Yeah," I laugh. "I was just thinking about the universe."

"You're always thinking about the universe."

"Well, the universe is full of mystery!"

"Yes, but the apple is ready to eat."

"Oh yeah—the apple." The once-red apple is now skinless and white. "Apples turn white when you peel them . . ."

"No duh," Walnut says. "But then if you leave them out overnight they turn red again. It's like they get rusty."

"Ah—do we have symmetry here as well? If you leave them out long enough, will they get all shiny again, too?"

"I doubt it! Not that I've tried . . ."

"It would be a waste to leave an apple out like that."

"Gosh, you're really taking your time eating tonight, Dad."

"Got it, got it."

The final countdown. The ninth inning of feeling like a housewife. I jam the last of the boiled vegetables and pickles into my mouth with the remainder of my rice and chew, my tongue and esophagus working in tandem to launch the food down my throat and into the depths of my body. My thoughts follow the food into the infinite expanse within me, while my hands place my chopsticks on the table. *Click*. They make a perfect line next to my teacup.

"Gochisō-sama."

Walnut stops eating her piece of apple.

"That's right—I was thinking about 'gochisō-sama.'"

She adjusts her posture in her chair.

"Wow," she says. "We got really off course there for a while."

"We weren't off course, honey. We were just having our dinner."

"Yeah, but do they say something like 'gochisō-sama' in other countries? You really don't know?"

"I'm as stumped as you. At least, I don't think I've noticed them saying anything in foreign movies."

"That's because movies never get to the 'gochisō-sama' part. They always switch to another scene when there's a pause in the conversation."

"Either that or they start fighting. Or somebody bursts into tears."

"Yeah, they can't just show a regular meal, can they. I guess movies won't help solve 'The Mystery of Gochisō-Sama.'"

"Maybe they don't say anything at all?"

"They can't just leave the table without saying something."

"True, true. And they pray before their meals—'Amen' or whatever."

"Just like we say 'itadakimasu.'"

"I guess they finish eating and clank down their knives and forks and . . ."

"And what do they say?"

"Man, I don't know . . ."

"They must say something."

"'Thank you,' maybe?"

"No way!"

"'Bye bye'?"

"You're just being silly, now."

"Honestly, I'm as curious as you are. But I'm also curious about how to reply."

"Reply?"

"Yeah. Like, say you've finished eating dinner and said your 'gochisō-sama.' What comes next? I'm never sure how to reply, and it always feels a little awkward."

"Now that you mention it . . . Gochisō-sama . . . What comes next . . . Gochisō-sama . . . 'Okay.' I think the correct reply is 'okay.'"

"You're right. I usually wind up saying 'okay.' But a simple 'okay' still feels inadequate. 'Okay' doesn't quite rise to the occasion, you know what I mean?"

"'Gochisō-sama . . . Okay.' You're right. 'Okay' doesn't take up enough space or something. It doesn't have any symmetry."

I stack up my dishes and carry them off to the kitchen. Walnut follows after with her own stack. I twist the spigot and water spurts out. The dishes slicken under the stream, the white ones turning white again and the blue ones turning blue. I stack them on the dish rack in their original glossy state, droplets of water sliding down the curves of their backs.

"A housewife," says Walnut, grinning up at me.

"Damn right I'm a housewife."

I untie my apron and give her a little pat on the head.

"But we're not a symmetric family," she says.

"We're not?"

"No—we don't have a mother."

"We sure don't. You've only got the one parent. But your dad is a housewife, so . . ."

"Yeah. I guess you make a symmetry all by yourself."

"That's right. I'm a walking symmetry over here. But you know what? You make a symmetry, too, Walnut."

"How am I a symmetry . . . ?"

"Well, you're not married yet, are you?"

"Psh! Of course not, silly."

"Well . . ."

"Ah I see. Our family is one kid and one adult. Like those two dots, one above the other. A colon. Wait—not a colon, more like an exclamation point."

The shape of an exclamation point materializes in both of our heads as we stand there in the kitchen.

!

We look at each other in unison.

!

We're not actually seeing the exclamation point with our eyes; we're looking at it with some other part of our heads. But I can tell we're both visualizing the same shape.

!

I think back to the first day I took Walnut to kindergarten. This was the day we became a single-parent household. Up until that point Walnut had lived with two parents: a man and a woman arranged in a sort of V-shaped symmetry—a wedge held together only by the child they shared.

Eventually this rusty old wedge began creaking and cracking until at last it split apart, the remaining pieces left standing there like an exclamation mark. It had never occurred to me that this exclamation mark might constitute a symmetry of its own. I had never thought of these two points as part of the same piece of punctuation. At the time, I just felt like a pregnant smelt, leaping out of the water, its belly swollen with roe.

"Goodnight, Dad."

"Goodnight, Walnut."

"Hey—that was an easy reply."

"Sure was."

"It's a symmetry."

"Haha. You're still on the symmetry thing, eh?"

"Goodnight!"

"Nighty-night."

I leave the kitchen, head to my bedroom, and switch on the desk lamp. I pour a little whiskey over ice and sip it slowly. Night time. Off in the distance, I catch faint intimations of Walnut getting ready for bed. I pick up the pencil that I use for work and think about housewife arms. The arms that housewives use for shopping. Bent ninety degrees at the elbow, a grocery bag hanging from the forearm. The telltale carraige of a housewife. At some point, that arm was superimposed over my own. I still remember standing in the produce aisle of the supermarket and noticing my arm in that distinct configuration. I felt like I was metamorphosing into a mollusk or something.

The arms of men don't usually assume this pose. When men carry things, they let their arms hang down, or sling their burden over one shoulder. When there's a lot to carry, men clench things against their chests. Men don't dangle grocery bags from forearms crossed in front of their bodies. It still feels weird to me. I still find these male arms strange.

I pour some more whiskey over ice and sip at it slowly. Night time. The pencil drops from my right hand. The whole world is aslumber. In the quiet of our home, an exclamation point drifts off to sleep.

◉⊙◎

"Gochisō-sama," says Walnut, clanging her knife and fork down on the table. Tonight we're eating out. We went to the bookstore for the first time in ages, then window-shopped through the shoe outlet, the stationer, the hardware store, and a pet shop, at which point it was too late to make dinner, so we ended up eating out at an American-style diner. I ordered a Salisbury steak. Walnut got a pork sauté. The whole flavor profile is so different from what we're used to eating that our stomachs, while full, are feeling a little uneasy. I'm done with my steak and sipping water—in other words, I've already said my gochisō-sama. But when Walnut finally submits her own gochisō-sama, I echo her for posterity:

"Okay. Gochisō-sama."

That's been our method lately. Walnut wipes her little lips with a napkin.

"Knives and forks are shaped different, but you hold them with both hands, so I guess that's a kind of symmetry. Right, Dad?"

"You're back on the symmetry thing, eh? Yeah—I guess there's a symmetry to that."

"Eating with both hands is kind of tricky, but I've started to get the hang of it."

"You sure have. You're a natural two-hander. You look like you're carving a pretty little sculpture there."

"Psh. A sculpture."

"But it does feel awkward to eat fish like white people, with a knife and fork."

"I don't think I've ever tried."

"Eating fish with a knife and fork ruins the whole experience. It feels like you're just mashing everything up."

"They don't go together, do they—fish and forks."

"Yeah. Fish was made for chopsticks."

"But I heard white people can't use chopsticks."

"Weird, right? Chopsticks are perfectly symmetric. It should be easy."

"Yeah, chopsticks are a symmetry. But you don't hold them with both hands. They're a symmetry, but a symmetry that you hold in one hand."

"Ooh, that's nice. Symmetry that you hold in one hand. Sounds like you've got a delicate little jewel in your palm."

"Yeah, an invisible jewel."

"A map made from precious stones or something. Paper made from gems."

"Super lightweight. Like you're holding air."

"Not something white people would be into."

"White people eat beef all the time."

"Eating with a knife and a fork means you have to use both hands. It makes you feel like you're eating with your entire body."

"Full-body symmetry."

"Whoa . . . Yeah . . . Full-body symmetry."

"And in Japan we have one-handed symmetry."

"But you know, eating one-handed, with chopsticks—it makes you feel like you're drawing a picture or practicing penmanship."

"I guess so. Yeah. It does kind of feel like you're doing calligraphy. It's basically food calligraphy."

"Ha. Food calligraphy! But I bet if you said 'food calligraphy' in front of a white person, they'd probably think it was some deep metaphysical thing."

"Metaphysical."

"Even saying 'metaphysical' makes me embarrassed."

"But it's true. Using a knife and fork with both hands makes eating feel more like a sport."

A family of four is dining at the next table. They arrived after us, and aren't quite done with their meal. Walnut keeps casting enquiring glances in their direction. She's waiting for a certain moment. I'm waiting for it, too. There are two kids, and the older one looks like she's just about done. She clanks down her fork and says:

"Gochisō-sama."

Walnut's eyes widen, staring at me. I freeze, too. We're both hanging on their next word. What comes next? What is the correct reply?

Their mother has already finished eating and is sipping coffee from a mug. She sets her mug on the table, gently smiles, and says:

"Okay."

I knew it. It was "okay" all along. Without a word, Walnut and I bring our eyes together and share a silent nod—the two of us in perfect symmetry.

oyster season

THE OYSTERS HAVE ARRIVED. *Well, crap*—I drop my pencil. I guess I can forget about finishing any work today. The pencil lands on my desk and clatters sideways. My desk must be a few degrees from plumb because the pencil keeps clacking until it plunks onto the floor, where it continues to roll. And then it keeps on rolling, and rolling, and rolling—long after it should have slowed to a stop. I just sit there gawking at it, mouth agape like a jug of saké. Or maybe I'm only gawking in my mind. In my mind, the pencil continues rolling, one anemic clack at a time, on the verge of disappearing altogether.

A sheet of carbon paper is still stuck to my fingers. It's the shipping form: air mail from Hiroshima. These oysters got on a plane at Hiroshima International Airport and took a direct flight to Tokyo. The delivery driver opened the door, handed me the receipt, and closed the door again. The vague smell of outside air still lingers around the cardboard box.

I look at the wall calendar. December. Wintertime. My whole

head snaps into an acute awareness of the season. My body has long since bid adieu to summer, bumbled through fall, and waded its way knee-deep into winter. But apparently my head has been asleep at the wheel this whole time, because now a second winter has arrived, right in the middle of the first.

It's been like this for the last five years. It was winter that first time. And it was winter the second time as well. For five years now, come winter, oysters have been arriving in the mail.

The pencil continues to clatter around in my head.

I'm still clutching the receipt. My whole body is frozen there in front of the box of oysters, posed for a commemorative photo. The box is the camera. Its shutter snapped open for the photo, but now it doesn't seem like it wants to shut again.

In actuality, this "camera" is packed with a morass of raw oysters. And raw oysters are, of course, raw. Left to their own devices, they will spoil as fast as they can. They eat time, growing bloated with each passing minute. It's been a good half an hour since the delivery driver set them down and hurried off. Half an hour spent in reverie. Half an hour devoured by oysters.

I peel the receipt from my fingers and place it on my desk. This is no time for reverie. These oysters need to be eaten as soon as possible. I feel like the starting pistol has just been fired at the local speed-eating contest. I'm facing a big deadline at work, but all that is out the window now. Come tomorrow, these oysters will be a little more spoiled, and even more spoiled the day after that. Even after you put them in the fridge, you can still feel them in there, gently festering away. This is the horror of raw oysters.

I pick up the phone and call the Chairman. The Chairman of the Board of Oyster Eaters. Our annual Chairman. The phone purrs a couple of times before I heard the click of someone picking up their own phone.

"Golden Treasure Herbal. How may I help you?"

"I'd like to speak with the Chairman?"

"Excuse me?"

"Oh. Sorry. I'm calling for Mr. Tanaka. Hitoshi Tanaka."

Golden Treasure is the name of the herbal medicine company where Chairman Tanaka works. Tanaka used to be a student of mine. He started working at Golden Treasure part-time between classes, then stayed on after graduation. At some point he transitioned to a full-time post.

"Mr. Tanaka is in a manager's meeting right now, but he should be back by three . . ."

Tanaka is a manager now? He must have started taking the job a bit more seriously. Back when he was in school, he always played off the whole herbal thing as a joke. And now he's running the joint.

"Oh yeah? Well, uh, I guess I'll just try him again later."

"And who might I say is calling?"

"Me? Uh—I'm just a friend."

"Care to leave a message?"

"Oh, thanks, but . . . uh . . . I'll just call back."

I hang up the phone. Then I stand there for a moment, a commemorative photo all over again. I am posed before that raw shellfish camera, framed in its raw shellfish lens. I can feel the twinge of the oysters festering within. I better hurry up and call the third member of the Board. I grab the phone and hastily dial.

The Board of Oyster Eaters has three official members: me, the Chairman, and Hanada. In theory, Hanada should be eating the bulk of these oysters. After all, he's the one who ended up with the swollen face five years ago. It hurt just to look at him. Ultimately, he's the true protagonist of this tale.

The phone purrs again. This time I've dialed a different number. Again, I hear a click as someone picks up.

"Hello?"

"South Seas Press, how may I help you?"

South Seas is a manga publishing house. Hanada works there as an editor. But once upon a time, he, too, was a student of mine. In class, he spent the entire time drawing manga. South Seas published a few of his comics, and eventually he got offered a job as an editor.

"Hello? South Seas here . . ."

"Oh. Uh . . ."

"Teach? Is that you? How've you been?"

I still get called "Teach" by former students, though these days it's more of a nickname than anything else. Back when Tanaka and Hanada were still students, the age gap between us felt insurmountable. But then they both graduated, and as we continued to hang out over the years, this gap grew narrower and narrower. At some point, our respective relationships flipped into pure power dynamics. You know how sometimes a younger friend from college grows up to be a CEO and decides to hire a few of their older buddies from school? But when everyone goes out drinking, the older crowd still kind of talks down to their younger friend, even though that person is technically their boss? That's basically what's happened here.

"Hey, Teach? You still there?"

"Oh—yeah. You been busy?"

"Sure, I guess. We got a new issue coming out, so it's gonna be trench warfare around here for the next couple of days . . ."

"Man, sorry to hear. Trench warfare, eh?"

"Pretty much. How about you? What's new?"

Hanada sounds pretty relaxed for someone so busy. I picture him with the phone squeezed between an ear and shoulder, hands free to fuss with pencils and scissors as he finishes up various bits of detail work. He probably shifted into this mode the moment he realized it was me. The sound of my voice let him know that this wouldn't be a work-related call, and he immediately resigned himself to a long and meandering conversation. He's listening to my voice the way you might listen to the radio: all his attention focused on his hands, so that his voice, conversely, assumes a relaxed and lolling tone.

"The, uh . . . ahem . . . the oysters have arrived."

"What?"

I can sense him stop whatever he's doing. But I repeat myself, just in case:

"You know. The oysters. They're here."

"The oysters . . . right."

Hanada goes quiet. I don't think he's working anymore. He, too, must have dropped his pencil. It's probably clattering over the surface of his desk. I bet it is. I bet it's rolling over to the edge and plunking onto the floor. And now it's continuing to roll across the floor while Hanada sits there gaping like an empty jug of saké. Of course I can't actually hear any of this. It's just something I intuit over the phone.

"Hello?"

The pencil is still rolling along in slow motion on the other end of the line.

"You still there?"

"Uh—yeah?"

"I like said: the oysters have arrived."

"They've . . . arrived . . ."

"They've arrived."

"So the oysters have arrived . . ." I imagine Hanada looking at his wall calendar. "It's winter . . . already . . . ?"

I knew it!

"Yep—winter already."

"Man, did the oysters have to arrive today of all days?"

"I know, I know. But they're here. What can you do?"

"Sheesh."

"Well? Do we eat them tonight? I guess we could get together tomorrow—I'm pretty sure they'll hold up for another day."

"Yeah . . . Tonight's gonna be tricky . . ."

"I get it. These oysters—they fly into town unannounced like: *Eat us immediately.* I bet they'll last another day or two."

"Yeah . . . Right . . ."

I can tell Hanada is on the fence. He's got the phone sandwiched between his ear and shoulder while his hands rest squarely on the fence. If South Seas is engaged in trench warfare for the next few days, then tomorrow night probably won't be an opportune time to enjoy oysters either. But the oysters . . . the oysters are raw.

"I mean, they're raw oysters, so . . ."

"I know, I know."

"They're just sitting here, proactively going bad."

"I get it, I get it. I'm just trying to think. Phew . . ."

"Me, I just threw in the towel. The moment the oysters arrived, I resigned myself to my fate. What can you do? Work goes straight out the window. Who would have imagined that raw oysters possessed such horrifying power?"

"What about the Chairman?"

"I tried calling. Apparently 'the manager' is out of the office at the moment."

"The manager? Tanaka?"

"That's right. Manager."

"Tanaka? A manager?"

"That's what they said."

"Huh. Maybe he's got better social skills than we gave him credit for."

"Yeah, looks like he managed to scrounge up some social skills after all."

"Man . . . still . . . I just don't know . . . Tomorrow might be better . . ."

"Tomorrow then?"

". . ."

"Tell you what: I'll call you back later. In the meantime, I gotta get these oysters into the fridge. I can't believe I let them sit out this long!"

I hang up the phone. The oysters are still sitting where the delivery driver left them. I'm flirting with disaster here; I've got to get these puppies on ice.

I lift the mass of organic matter with both hands. It has the heft of wetness. The entire package is soggy with rawness. A postcard-sized logo of the Hiroshima oyster farm decorates the top of the box. Next to the logo is a label, which reads "RAW OYSTERS," followed by "2kg," and then the sender's name: "KAZUMA MORI."

In the blue indentations of the carbon paper, I can feel the pressure of the hand that penned these letters. Mori is from Hiroshima. Five years ago, he, too, was one of my students. Staring at his name like this, I feel like I'm looking at the name engraved on a tombstone. Which sounds a little macabre, since Mori is still alive and well. Somehow, he's still doing fine, in spite of . . . well . . . in spite of everything.

A pencil starts rolling around in my head again. The nub of a used eraser starts tumbling around in there as well. Hold on. No time for pencils. Get it together, man.

I lug the box into the kitchen, squat down in front of the fridge, and pop through the plastic string with a pair of scissors. Freed from its binds, the box relaxes a bit. I flip open its slackened flaps to reveal two white styrofoam bricks sealed with yellow packing tape. Two kilograms gross: one per brick. I extract one of the bricks and slide my fingernail over the surface of the tape until I find an edge. I give the tape a yank, and it screeches away from the styrofoam, sending ripples of sound through the kitchen.

I lift the lid from the brick and frigid air rushes out. I've always been impressed by the insulating power of styrofoam. Lighter than paper, it's carried the chilly air of Hiroshima all the way to Tokyo without spilling a drop.

A soft, silvery bag appears on the heels of this icy breeze. I've reached the final layer of packaging. Inside is nothing but moisture and oysters. I gently extract the bag using both hands. This is hazardous material, after all. The metallic bag blobs around like quicksilver. The oysters, those blubbery anarchists, are still asleep inside. I've got a glob of nitroglycerin in my hands. An icy brick of sleeping explosives. A bag packed with raw organic matter, just waiting to go bad. Unprocessed biomass, courting disaster . . . I'm still staring at this strange object when I hear a jingling sound. It's sound of the bell that my daughter, Walnut, wears on her backpack. She's in the first grade.

"I'm hoooome!" I hear Walnut say. "How come I'm so late, today is, um, my friend Aya and I stayed after school to study, and on the way home Aya said she didn't want to walk on the dirt road, so I took the road by the bakery with her, and we ran into a boy from class . . ."

Walnut's already thrown herself into a long excuse for being late. She must have spent the whole walk home concocting this tale, the little bell jingling with each step. And now her excuse comes panting out in little puffs.

But Walnut stops short when she notices the object in my hands.

"What's that?"

"This? This here is a bomb. A bomb on ice."

"What? A bomb? Stop being silly, Dad—you're always joking."

"Haha. But really, it's dangerous. This is raw organic matter."

"Oh!"

"You remember what these are?"

"Yeah—they come in the mail, right?"

"Exactly! These are oysters. Raw oysters."

"Raw oysters?"

"Yeah, oysters. From the ocean. You've had oysters before, Walnut. Remember?"

"Oh . . . I thought oyster was a kind of sauce . . ."

She may not be old enough to remember, but Walnut has been eating these oysters with us every winter for a few years, now. This will be the first year we have them together as a single-parent household.

"Now I remember! We had them in a hot pot, right?"

"Yup. A hot pot with vegetables and tofu and everything. A miso-oyster hot pot."

"At our old house, right? And Mr. Hanada and the Chairman were all there."

"Ha ha, exactly! Except the time you're remembering wasn't at our old house. Last year I took you to the Chairman's house, and we ate there."

"Oh . . ." Walnut says absent-mindely as she heaves her backpack onto a chair. Then she opens a drawer and begins selecting a series of seemingly random objects—little cardboard boxes and tin cans full of rocks. She's off to play Shoopsy at her friend Aya's house. I know "Shoopsy" is the name of a game they play together, but its rules remain shrouded in mystery.

"Off to play a little Shoopsy with Aya?"

"Bingo," Walnut says, her arms loaded with knickknacks.

She's clearly in a rush to leave, but I notice her eyeing the oysters.

"Hey, Dad?" she asks. "Where do the oysters come from, every year?"

"They're from Mr. Mori—remember him? The guy with the camera?"

"We have a camera, too."

"Yeah, but Mr. Mori's camera is for work. He's a professional photographer."

"How come he keeps sending us oysters?"

"Well, that's uh . . . Umm . . ." I try to come up with an easy explanation, but it's the kind of thing that takes a lot of explaining, even for adults. "Well . . . You see . . ."

"*Well . . . You see . . .*" Walnut's impression of me is spot-on as she throws on her sneakers and dashes off to Aya's.

Quiet falls over the house in the wake of Hurricane Walnut. The air, kicked up and roiled by Shoopsy fever, now settles back down over the kitchen. My ears begin to open up again. The refrigerator's motor stops. I can hear my own breathing. The groan of a garbage truck stretches out like noodles over some distant road.

I gently open the door of the refrigerator, silver bag in hand. Inside, a half dozen swords are hanging from the ceiling. Their tapered blades gleam brightly.

I startle, slam the refrigerator door shut, leap to my feet.

Through the kitchen window I can see my neighbor's roof and TV antenna. I count its erect arms: One . . . two . . . Nothing seems to be out of order. I'm still a little spooked, but thinking rationally now. What just happened? Did somebody break into our house? I was home all day yesterday. In the evening, Walnut and I took a quick trip to the store, but we definitely locked the doors on our way out. When we got home, I made fried rice and we ate it together. Then I locked the front door and checked all the windows. I even turned off the gas before going to bed. There's no way anybody could have snuck in. I must be hallucinating. Why would there be a bunch of swords in our fridge?

I stand there for a spell, the oysters still squishy in my hands. Then I open the refrigerator door—the portal to a winter day, years ago—and place the oysters inside.

I situate the oysters on the top shelf, right below the evaporator coils. Some sardines lie next to them, fast asleep. A brick of butter is sleeping as well. So, too, the tofu. Even the leftover rice is taking a nap. The yogurt simply sits there, while the pudding cups squat. The can of tomato juice stands at attention. The mayonnaise is likewise on its feet. Several beers are sort of huddled together, but they're all upright. The ketchup has crappy posture. *All right, everybody. Take care in there.*

I close the door again. But just before it closes completely, I catch another glimpse of those gleaming blades. I startle, try to stop the door, but it thumps shut before I can catch it. This isn't real. My mind is just playing tricks on me. Long, glistening icicles dangle down inside the refrigerator in my head. Icicles that I know from somewhere, years ago.

On TV—that's right. There was a brief period of time when these very same icicles were being broadcast around the clock. Whenever you flipped on the news, these absurdly long icicles would be glistening there on your cathode tube. What year was that again? The year our TVs relentlessly aired image after image of that cold and snowy winter? A three-story building perched awkwardly on a slope. Icicles, several meters long, dangling from its eaves. Riot police hosing down the building from dawn till dusk. The icicles growing longer and longer as they sprayed.

There was something sinister about those icicles. The way they dangled down like frozen entrails: small and large intestines, hanging from the eaves. It was as if the guts of a refrigerator had been scraped out and strung from the roof of that desolate building. From the moment you woke up until the moment you went to sleep, that same scene would be playing on repeat.

That same year, right after the icicles disappeared from our TV sets, I found myself sitting in the waiting room of a maternity ward, reading a newspaper. On the front of the newspaper was a picture of a hole, somewhere deep in the mountains. At the bottom of the hole lay human-shaped objects made of white rope. Several of them. Boldface lettering filled the face of the newspaper like a row of cavities:

UNITED RED ARMY LYNCHINGS

The word "lynchings" felt particularly raw, as if gingivitis had eaten away at the membrane around the type.

The waiting room was filled with newspapers like this. Everyone just sat there in silence. We had all been watching that same snowy scene on TV, and now it felt like we had each been given our own personal icicle. Someone had slipped icicles into our coat collars, and now they were slowly sliding down our backs. That was the autumn Walnut was born. I hardly spoke, took photographs instead.

Seven years have passed since then. Seven years later, it's just Walnut and me.

Quiet fills my ears. I'm squatting in front of the refrigerator, my back pressed against its door. The motor switches on with a click and begins to hum huskily. It's chilling itself again. I can hear the blades inside. They're growing longer and longer, their icy weight pressing against the oysters. The oysters shrink away from the frigid steel, huddling up in one corner. The sardines cower. The butter curls into fetal position. The leftover rice cringes. Everyone clusters together, their backs caressed by the icy breath hissing from the tips of the swords.

Inside this refrigerator is a little town, a town where the winters are colder than cold and a white chill shimmers over the streets, scrutinizing every surface. The blades grow longer and longer until they clink against a can of tomato juice. That's it. This sound. The clink of a can.

The clink of a can reverberates through the frozen town. It clatters off the refrigerator unit, the bottles of beer, the butter dish, the milk. Then it ricochets over to the pudding cup, where a two-year-old version of Walnut is perched. She sits stiff as a board, her eyes unmoving.

Clink . . . clink . . . clink . . . clink . . . The clatter of a tin can . . .

This town is where two-year-old Walnut lives. I trudge over to her, growing smaller and smaller with each step. By the time I reach her, I've shrunk to the size of a bug.

⊙⊙⊙

Hey—so, you know the sound an empty can makes when you kick it? *Clink, clatter, clatter . . .* A crumpled can of cola or beer, destined to get swept down a storm drain. Something about this can is just begging to be kicked. You're walking along and then the next thing you know:

Clink!

You're kicking the can. And as you continue to kick you realize that you're not just kicking the can—you're kicking the sound of the can.

Clink, clatter, clatter . . .

The city at night. This clink is clamoring through it. You're in the middle of Tokyo but there's hardly anybody around, because this is the Kanda district, and Kanda sleeps early. It's a college area, so when the lights go out at school, the whole neighborhood calls it a night. This happens in business districts, too.

And the concrete here in Kanda is really hard. I mean, all concrete is hard, but something about this concrete feels incredibly dense. Same difference, I know.

Clink, clatter, clatter . . .

It's nighttime in Kanda. A can is being kicked by a college kid. I'm the kid's teacher—I teach a class with the inscrutable name "Picture Class." I only have eight students, so it's more like a study hall. A study hall for adults. We meet once a week, starting at noon, and class lasts until nine at night. Somewhere along the way we get dinner and start drinking, so a lot of the time we don't finish until ten or eleven. It's the kind of class where getting a little drunk isn't frowned upon. I know this sounds unconventional, but whatever: I'm the teacher and I make the rules. I still teach the same class to this day.

But a few years back we had a bit of an incident. A terrible, scandalous incident. An incident that, to be honest, was an embarrassment to everyone involved. And now you get to hear all about it.

Clink, clatter, clatter . . .

The kicked can clatters across the concrete, coming to rest against a curb.

Clunk.

At which point someone else goes over to kick the crumpled can. It's nighttime and nobody's around, so they haul off and punt it.

Clang, clatter, clatter . . .

This is essentially a form of soccer, though without any explicit rules. One kid kicks the can, then another gives it a boot. Nobody has anywhere important to be, so a third kid comes and kicks it, too. This continues for a while, almost unconciously, until the can comes to rest under a parked car—

Clunk.

And with that, the game is over. At least we think it's over. An audible hush falls over Kanda.

Hush . . .

Everybody's attention turns elsewhere. Someone tries to make a quip.

Quip!

Not that there are many quips to be made. There never are, to be honest. So we continue walking toward the train station, silent aside from the occasional quip.

Quip!

Then, from somewhere far behind us, we detect the faint clang of a can.

Clang, clack, clink . . .

Peering down the dark street, we spy a distant straggler, trying to cajole the can back out. Apparently they really want to keep kicking the can, because they've squatted down next to the car and are thigh-deep beneath the chassis. It would be easy enough to just grab the can with their hands, but this kid is intent on kicking. Feet only.

Eventually they coax the can back into the open, then wind up and give it a swift crack.

Crack!

And we're back at it. Kicking the old can. Each kid waits their turn to kick, until at last we arrive at the first of many bars signifying our proximity to the train station.

The shutters are coming down over the door, and a handful of people stand outside, loudly debating the bill. One customer hovers over the gutter, puking.

Blerrrgh! Bleeccckt!

Even a sleepy college district like Kanda gets a little spicy around the station. The people outside the bar are clearly college students—we can tell at a glance. It's not like they're wearing letterman sweaters or anything, but we can tell. It may be the way they dress or the way they talk or something about their facial expressions. They all share a similar collegiate je ne sais quoi.

The kids from my Picture Class, on the other hand, exude an entirely different aura. They're a mismatched jumble to begin with, and nothing about them smells of "college." They play kick the can with unusual tenacity, for starters. Regular college students might play kick the can from time to time, but once the can goes under a car, it's game over for them.

Clang, clatter, clatter . . .

Meanwhile my students from Picture Class continue kicking until the bloody end. We persevere past several more bars and under an overpass until we arrive at the train station. And we keep taking turns kicking the can while everyone purchases tickets, at which point we file through the ticket gate, casually kicking as we go.

A flight of stairs stands between us and the platform, and here the game becomes a matter of sheer willpower. Grasping the can between our feet, we leap into the air, flinging it up the stairs with all our might. We grab the handrail for support, lowering our bodies like gymnasts on the parallel bars, whipping the can upward through the air.

Whip!

Businessmen hurrying to catch the last train shoot us dirty looks. To be honest, people have been staring daggers at us ever since we approached that first bar.

Stab! Stab!

But we're no longer just kicking this can for shits and giggles—we're kicking as if our lives depended on it. The other commuters clearly don't share our enthusiasm, but my students only seem to bask in their disapproving glances. Undaunted, they whip the can up the long station stairway and onto the platform, then straight onto a waiting train.

We all pile aboard, and then someone plants a foot on the crumpled can. We reach up for our respective straps, and with that, the game has arrived at its natural conclusion. Someone starts making quips again.

Quip!

Somebody else chuckles at the quip.

Hehehe . . .

Which, anyways. The incident I'd like to tell you about does not involve an errant can smacking into somebody's forehead or anything like that. The incident in question has nothing to do with cans at all. It takes place on an entirely different evening.

It was around ten at night, and we had already lost interest in cans. We were meandering toward the station, our lives no longer depending on kicking of any kind. If we came across a can, well, the most it warranted from us was a disinterested glance.

Glance . . .

Which is not to say that we had anything better to do. This was as fine a night as any to engage in a little kickery. It's just that nobody thought to give a can that first crack, so the kicking never commenced.

We'd all had a little extra to drink during class, and everybody was feeling looser than usual. One kid named Mori was feeling especially loose. So loose, in fact, that he broke into song.

While singing, he leapt up and snatched a cherry branch from the side of the road. Not a real branch—this was Tokyo, after all—but one of those plastic ornaments with cellophane blossoms that you see hanging from streetlights.

The whole scene felt deeply surreal: the empty street lined with fake pink flowers and gaudy green leaves; Mori leaping up mid-song to snatch a branch from a streetlight.

Snap!

Except the branch was plastic, so it didn't really snap. It simply tore off in a long, diagonal strip.

Rrrrrrip!

Blossoms and leaves dangled from the tattered branch in Mori's hand. This cracked us up, because it was funny to see plastic flowers going:

Flutter, flutter, flutter . . .

We were tickled by the whole scene, with the flowers fluttering softly under the streetlights. So tickled that we started egging Mori on.

Mori is one of those people who are kind of stocky but at the same time weirdly skinny, and he's always got this shit-eating grin on his face. He used to be a wrestler in high school, although he's kind of shy for an ex-wrestler. One time we were drinking at school and he did something called a "bridge," where you lie down face up and arch your back like a stone bridge so that the weight of your body is balanced on your head and toes. Mori made it look easy, but it's actually really hard to do. Apparently being able to do a bridge is proof that you are a bona fide wrestler.

At any rate, Mori took the cherry branch he'd expropriated from the streetlight and foisted it over his shoulder. Then he set off tap-dancing down the street, proud as a peacock.

Tappity-tap, tappity-tap . . .

None of us were ready to get quite as loose as Mori. We just watched and snickered and egged him on, the whole group slowly moving toward the station.

Mori spun around and strutted across the street—

Tappity-tap, tappity-tap . . .

—then came strutting back again. It was just like kicking a can, except that one of us had become the can and was kicking himself. And like our other games of kick the can, this one eventually brought us to Suidōbashi Station.

Mori tapped on over to the ticket machine—

Tappity-tap, tappity-tap . . .

—and dropped in a dollar coin into the coin slot:

Clatter-clatter . . .

The rest of us followed suit, smirking all the while:

Clatter-clatter, clatter-clatter . . .

And this is where things took a turn for the worse. Because there was a man standing by the ticket machine. Mori went dancing by him—

Tappity-tap, tappity-tap . . .

—tapping the man on the shoulder—

Tap . . .

—and greeting him jovially: "Nice weather we're having, sir!"

But as Mori continued sauntering on toward the gate, his plastic flowers got caught in the man's hair. That's when everything really took a turn for the worse.

The man turned toward Mori, revealing a long scar down his pale cheek. He shot Mori a knife-like glare—

Glint!

—which is when we realized that the man was standing with a few friends. Things had unequivocally taken a turn for the worse.

⦿⦿⦿

The front door clatters open and a voice comes hollering down the hall:

"Dad! Can you get my jump rope? It's next to my desk!"

It's Walnut. She and Aya must have finished playing Shoopsy and are moving on to jump rope. I glance at the other, two-year-old Walnut. She sits there in the fridge, stiff as a board, unblinking.

"Dad! My jump rope! Are you even home?!"

The uncertainty in her voice is audible.

"Listen . . ." she mumbles. "I'm gonna . . . So we can . . ."

She's talking to someone else. Aya must be with her. I get up and walk down the hall.

"Eek! Dad! You're home!"

"Of course I'm home. I wouldn't leave without telling you."

"I was yelling for you! To get my jump rope."

"I heard you. Sheesh."

"But you didn't answer . . ."

"Sorry, I'm kind of busy. I can't just be at your beck and call."

"Can you go get my jump rope? These shoes are really hard to get off."

Walnut and Aya must have sprinted all the way here, because they both look out of breath.

"Oh—hey, Aya!"

"Hi!" Aya smiles and continues panting.

"Dad! Can you get my jump rope already?!"

Walnut is trying to act bossy in front of her friend.

"Yeah, yeah, yeah. Stop being so bossy!"

She has turned into a straight line. When it's just the two of us, Walnut is more of a gentle curve, but when she's with her friends she snaps into a vector, plumb as a two-by-four, pointed straight at play. I go over to her desk and fetch the jump rope.

"Voilà," I say, handing her the rope.

"Voilà," she parrots. "Aya and I are going to play at the Airplane Park."

By the time the word "park" reaches my ears, the door is already shut. I guess I ought to be happy she remembered to close the door behind her. I stare at the door for a moment, then return to the kitchen. Not that I have any business in the kitchen, either. I've just instinctually circled back to where I was before the interruption, like a cat coming home for dinner. I squat back down in front of the refrigerator, my back pressed against its door. That winteriest of winter towns spreads out behind me. Two-year-old Walnut sits there on a pudding cup, stiff as a board. I am trudging through those frozen streets once more, my footsteps clattering across the concrete. Kanda at night. The shadow of Suidōbashi Station. A group of sillhouettes, huddled there behind the refrigerator door.

⦿⦿⦿

So Mori had tapped this guy's shoulder—

Tap!

—and the guy had turned to glare at him—

Glint!

—and at first it seemed like everything would be fine. We all mumbled our apologies and pushed Mori through the ticket gate.

Mumble, mumble . . .

We were worried that the guy might haul off and deck him. Mori, for his part, was so drunk that one of the other students had to help escort him to his train. He was still tap-dancing as he disappeared up the stairs, blissfully unaware that anything was awry.

Tappity-tap, tappity-tap . . .

Meanwhile the rest of us continued muttering nervously as we started toward our respective trains.

Mutter, mutter . . .

But of course it wasn't going to be that easy. The glinty man with the pallid face still had an axe to grind—

Grind, grit, grate . . .

—because he reached out and snatched of of my students by their collar.

Yank!

This student had nothing to do with the incident. The man had randomly grabbed one of the ten or so of us still standing around, and now he was shouting directly into their face:

"The fuck d'you think you're doing?"

Apparently he just wanted to know what the fuck we were doing. Except that none of us were capable of giving him a straight answer. That's why we spent so much time kicking cans around. None of us had the faintest idea what we were doing, much less how to fight. Nor were any of us assertive enough to declare:

"Well, XYZ, you see!"

The most we could conjure were vague suggestions:

"Well, I guess X . . . ? And maybe Y . . . ?"

Which wasn't going to cut it with this guy. Our assertions were so flaccid that we could feel him losing his appetite for a fight. For a moment, it seemed like the whole situation might defuse on its own.

But the glinty man was more tenacious than any of us had anticipated. He held my student's collar with one persistent fist and refused to let go. His pale face glistened. None of us knew how to properly protest or apologize.

Here is where Hanada comes in.

The name "Hanada" literally means "flowerbed," and this particular Hanada is a bit eccentric in that he doesn't experience fear. Or better said: the entire concept of fear doesn't make sense to him. He knows what pain is, but he claims he's never felt scared of anything. Because of this, he doesn't fear death. Which, by extension, means that he isn't worried about getting punched. Unfortunately, he's not a tough guy by any means, which makes it all the worse. According to Hanada, pain is just something you ride out, like a wave, which makes what happened next even worser still, because Hanada just trotted right up to the man—

Trot, trot, trot . . .

—and proceeded to articulate the Truth of the Matter. To wit: a drunk kid tapped you on your shoulder; stop making a fuss about it.

The Truth of the Matter was, in fact, true. But it was precisely this trueness that made matters so much worse.

Glint!

The pale face glared again. Its glimmer made it plain as day: the Truth of the Matter wasn't going to be of any help here. Which is why we had been trying to apologize our way out of the situation. But now that the Truth of the Matter had arrived on the scene, there was no turning back. Our fate was sealed. All the man had to do was ask for confirmation—*Stop making a fuss?*—and we'd be on his turf. The turf of a professional. In terms of starting fights, this man was clearly a technician.

"Stop making a fuss?" the man asked. "Then maybe we ought to take this to the police station and talk it out like gentlemen."

The phrase "police station" was the killer here. Once you've aligned yourself with the Truth of the Matter, the only reply you're left with is: *That sounds reasonable.* Hanada had slapped the Truth of the Matter card down on the table and we were stuck playing with it for the rest of the hand.

Slap!

And so Hanada duly agreed with the man, at which point the man's pals all began glinting too.

Glimmer, gleam!

They all started walking, smirks lurking in the corners of their eyes.

Smirk!

The north exit of Suidōbashi Station. The opposite side. Facing Kōrakuen Ballpark. While the Kanda side of the station stays bustling and lively late into the night, the stadium side gets dark and empty and eerily quiet after sundown.

Hushhhh . . .

The further we got from the station, the more ominous it all felt. A chill crept down the nape of my neck. I felt like I was walking into the depths of a refrigerator. There wouldn't be any police stations where we were headed. But if these gentlemen insisted on going to the police, then, as Team Truth of the Matter, we were obliged to comply.

And so we trudged along on heavy, reluctant legs: Hanada's legs, Tanaka's legs, and my own pair of rusty pipes. I'd sent the other students home—I was their teacher, after all. They'd looked worried, but I'd put my foot down—

Stomp!

—and eventually they'd given in.

I started wondering whether everyone had made it home all right, and as I was thinking about this I noticed another group of people plodding along in the same direction:

Shuffle, shuffle, shuffle . . .

What were the chances that another group would be headed toward the same dark and empty stadium at this hour of night? It seemed highly unlikely. Out of the corner of my eye, I noticed that they all wore the same buzz cut. Then, from even deeper in the corner of that eye, I saw that they were all carrying karate uniforms, folded in neat little bundles. I returned my gaze to the center of my eyes and stared ahead. The group of glinting men trudged on ahead of me.

Glimmer, glitter, glint . . .

Oh no, I thought to myself. *We're in uncharted territory now.* The sound of my footsteps grew even more reluctant.

Plod, plod, plod . . .

The broad, black road stretched darkly out before us, dangling vacantly into the void.

Dangle, dangle . . .

We had arrived at the deepest part of a refrigerator, and our escorts weren't about to let us back out. We passed over a murky drainage basin, cut across an empty intersection, and found ourselves in an empty parking lot.

The parking lot was as dark as a beach at night. The feeling of "Here we are at last!" lost the final "at last" and became a simple "here we are . . ." Then it dropped the "we are" and became a mere "here . . ." Finally the "here" fell away, leaving us with a lone ellipsis:

". . ."

Taking our disagreement to the police station had been the correct course of action. The location of the police station, however, was entirely incorrect.

Kōrakuen Ballpark in the dead of night. Standing on the empty pavement at the base of the stadium's sheer cliff. Massive concrete pillars towered before us, buttressing the bleachers. We were locked in a giant concrete room with only one exit: straight up into the night sky. Behind us loomed an iron fence—

Loom!

—on the other side of which ran an asphalt road. Every so often a car would come snarling by—

Vrruuuuoooommm . . .

—its headlights flickering between the fence slats as it passed.

Flicker, flicker, flicker . . .

During the day, this parking lot was probably mobbed with lines of people trying to buy tickets. And now here we were, gathered on that same slab of concrete. As my eyes grew accustomed to the dark, I began to make out the figure of Hanada. He was standing in the middle of the empty lot, completely agleam. "Completely agleam" makes Hanada sound extremely glamorous, but what I mean is that he was surrounded by glinting men. About twenty of them, shuffling into a semicircle around him.

Shuffle, shuffle, shuffle . . .

Then they all just stood there, legs splayed, karate uniforms dangling from their fists. It looked like a goddamn movie. Not even a movie—a page from a goddamn manga. And to the extent that I was scared for my life, I could also feel a part of my brain getting a little goofy.

Wobble, wobble . . .

But that was only one little wobbly part of my brain. The rest of it was completely paralyzed with fear. Meanwhile the other cells in my body were running around in a frenzy. I couldn't tell if I was hot or cold anymore. A column of ice crept in through my collar. One of those long icicles was sliding down my back. It slipped slowly southward, melting into my underwear. Light from a passing car flickered over the semicircle of men, momentarily turning them into a row of black-clad riot police, aluminum shields all aglimmer—

Glimmer, glimmer, glimmer . . .

◎⊙◎

"Brrrrrring . . . Brrrrrring . . ."

The phone rings. I peel my back off the refrigerator door, shuffle over to my bedroom, and pick up the phone.

"Hello?"

It's probably the Chairman. Except that I declined to leave my name with his secretary, so it can't be him.

"Hello?"

Maybe it's Hanada.

"Hello?"

Or even Mori—who knows?

"Hello . . . ?"

But the person on the other end stays mum.

"Hello? Who is this?"

Maybe they have the wrong number. But whoever it is, they aren't hanging up. Did they call just to sit there, listening to my voice? Or maybe something important came up while the phone was still ringing. This happens a lot on radio programs for kids, when really young listeners call in but then lose interest mid-call and wander off to do something else.

"Hello?"

The person on the other end still won't speak. But some curious form of stubbornness is preventing me from hanging up. Women, of course, get phone calls like this all the time—usually from perverts.

"Hello . . . ?"

Still no reply. Not a peep. A phone call on mute. Long-distance sign language. An invisible body, cramped in a faraway phone booth, bating its breath. The body begins to shimmer and wiggle into view, part by unseen part. That same faded sweater she used to wear. The oversized collar of her shirt. And then her ear, like a piece of butterscotch candy, pressed to the receiver. That oppressive silence. A silence like butterscotch, too hard to ever melt away . . . *Buzz, crackle . . . Brrrrr, crack . . .* Static rasps from deep within the phone, the sound of fingernails on the bottom of a skillet.

Buzz, Brrrr . . . Crickle, crack . . .

I know this sound, this static. An iron bug is wriggling around in there: way down on the other end of the phone line. Its feelers reach out through miles of cable, all the way to my own receiver, where they scratch at my eardrum.

Brrrr, crackle . . . Tick, titter . . .

There's something almost nostalgic about this sound. I used to hear it all the time, crackling around the edges of my telephone conversations.

I first heard it around 1970. According to a friend who was versed in surveillance, this was the sound of a police wiretap. Apparently this particular kind of static was an indication that the feds had bugged your phone. I wasn't a member of any anti-government organizations, but it did seem like this crackling always showed up during calls from friends who were adjacent to such groups. Even it it was all just my imagination, we later learned that a lot of us had, in fact, been bugged.

Buzz, crackle . . . Crinkle, bzzzz . . .

The caller still hasn't spoken. We're being surveilled before we've even started talking. Even if the cops were interested in my conversations, this wasn't the sort of call from which they could glean anything. I'm basically just an answering machine, here. Actually, no—it's the other way around: an answering machine has called me. An answering machine has showed up on my doorstep with a wiretap, special delivery. What is this, sketch comedy? Give me a break.

"Give me a break!"

I intend to shout this as I slam the phone down, but my words come out closer to a whisper. Whoever the caller is, they have succeeded in creeping me out. I'm not sure they even heard me. And who is the "they" here, anyway? It's been forever since I encountered that strange static. I can't remember the last time. Maybe the cop in charge of eavesdropping ran out of work, got bored, and decided to call me for practice. Nobody's doing anything that warrants snooping anymore. The cop has put a lid over his receiver and is just sitting there in silence. Sitting there with a lid on his phone, an icicle tickling his back . . . There's something deeply disturbing about a silent phone call. I can't shake the image of that woman's butterscotch ear, pressed up against the other end of the line. It stays with me long after I've clanged the receiver back onto its cradle. All I can do is wait for this feeling to crumple up into a ball and toss itself into the garbage can.

Again I find myself wandering back to the kitchen like a cat. The white door of the refrigerator is primly shut. Behind it lies a winter cityscape. Cold concrete clatters beneath my feet.

◎⊙◎

Kōrakuen Ballpark in the dead of night, the stadium looming over us. A sheer concrete cliff with nothing but pitch-black sky above. Dim lights from the distant city cast faint human shadows across the pavement. Faceless shapes, frozen in place.

Hush . . .

The glinty man and Hanada were exchanging words. I couldn't hear exactly what they were saying, but I could catch snatches of Hanada's voice.

"Clearly you won't be satisfied until you hit someone . . . So hurry up and hit me . . . I'd like to get this over with . . ."

He sounded like a tiny insect chirping.

Chirp, chirp . . .

A tiny insect pleading to be hit. It absolutely blew my mind. Hanada intended to play the Truth of the Matter card all the way to the bloody end. He truly didn't experience fear the way others did. This had to be frustrating for the glinty man, who'd cornered his prey only to find it completely inedible.

Thud.

I heard a dull thud, and Hanada keeled over.

Thud, thud, thud, thump . . .

The man started kicking at Hanada where he lay. Hanada winced at each kick, covering his vulnerable areas and waiting for it all to be over.

He had gone full-on Gandhi. A Japanese Ghandi, rolling around on the pavement. By the time the glinty man had landed half a dozen good kicks, there wasn't much left to kick. Each subsequent thud just made the man's violence seem all the more absurd. It sure looked like it hurt, though. I tried to say something to Tanaka, who was standing next to me, but my throat only allowed a tiny gurgle out—

Gurgle . . .

My own body hadn't been turned into Gandhi's yet. It merely shook and shivered. Sure, Hanada was in a lot of pain, but I had fear to deal with. I even started to worry about whether Tanaka had noticed all my shaking.

A man in a black suit walked over to us, wearing a smile. Even in the dark, I could read his smile loud and clear. It said: *Hey, I'm just an innocent bystander here.* He asked me what was wrong. *Was something bothering me? Could I tell him what was the matter?* He seemed affable, as if he truly wanted to help, his genial tone calming my nerves for a moment. I wanted to answer him, but my throat still felt like a drainpipe with a rat stuck in it. When I finally got a few words out, it just sounded like:

S . . . s . . . s . . . stammer.

How was I supposed to explain or plead our case while Hanada was over there getting the shit kicked out of him? I could sense my ability to convey meaning with language crumbling inside me, my words stiffening like drying clay. The man, who had initially seemed so gentle, suddenly burst into anger.

"Fuck this guy!" he shouted. "Stammering like an idiot, wasting my time! He's the fucking worst of the lot."

So this guy was on the other team, too. Judging by the black suit he wore, he was probably their boss.

Meanwhile, Hanada's utter lack of resistance to being kicked was making the guy kicking him look more and more vile with each subsequent thud. Sure, this glinty man was used to playing the villain, but this wasn't even a fight. He looked like he was beating up a small, defenseless child.

Which only made matters worse. You can't really get all the punching out of your system unless the person you're punching tries to punch you back. That's why the guy in the suit had tried to talk me up: to suss out the thread of the fight.

But he was sussing up the wrong tree, because the most I could offer him was a tremulous stammer:

S . . . s . . . s . . . stammer, s . . . stammer . . .

When the gentle approach failed, the man changed tactics and started hurling insults at me. He questioned my manhood, my morals, sussing at me from every possible angle. But the threads in me had all hardened up. I was a ball of twine coated in glue. You couldn't suss a loose end out of me if you scraped with your fingernails.

Over in the center of the lot, the glinty man was trying the same tactic. He stood over Hanada, sussing away: "Stand up, bitch! Be a man and fight back!" But Hanada was all out of loose threads, too. There was no way he was going to try and be a man.

Hush!

All at once, a hush fell over the semicircle of men.

Hush!

It was the same sort of ominous hush as earlier, but lacking the authority of the first. The glinty man had stopped kicking and was resting his legs. The man in the black suit wandered back and forth between me and the semicircle of men, jawing off as he walked.

"Well, well, well," he sighed.

"Hehehe," he chuckled.

"For chrissakes . . ."

"Unbelievable . . ."

"Yeesh . . ."

It felt like the intermission at a movie—like I should try and run to the bathroom real quick. Maybe even stop for some popcorn on the way back? Either way, I needed to hurry, because at any moment another hush might fall over the audience, and who knew what the second act might hold . . . At some point, while I was thinking about all this, the semicircle of karate kids vanished. They just up and left. I imagine they were from the martial arts team at Japan University. They were probably on their way home from practice when they struck up a conversation with the glinty men at the station. Then the whole incident with Mori took place, and one of the glinty men was like: *Why don't you kids tag along and see how we work? If you get lucky, you might even get in a little hands-on practice.*

Except they didn't luck out, because Hanada pulled a Gandhi

and ruined the whole mood. The glinty men had probably told them all to head home. *Nothing to see here. But hey—give us a call tomorrow. We might have a job for you.*

Only a half a dozen men remained, at this point. They stood around in jackets and tracksuits. Quiet fell over the scene once more.

Hush . . .

Eventually a few more men left, until only three remained: the glinty man, some guy in a suit, and a man in a tracksuit. The guy in the suit wasn't the same one from before. He was wearing a brown jacket, which probably meant his rank was lower than the guy in the black suit. Still, he was clearly the highest-ranking member of the three remaining men.

Hanada had gone completely silent. Silent and still. But the glinty man still seemed antsy. Deep down, he probably wanted to be done with the whole ordeal too, but he still had all this energy to burn. His muscles were dancing around in his body. As he paced back and forth, I realized that he was much smaller and younger than I had imagined, his vitality seething just beneath his skin. It came boiling up out of his eyes.

Glare . . .

"Where'd the drunk motherfucker go?" he demanded, trying a new tactic. "He's a friend of yours, right?"

For our part, we stuck to denying culpability: *We don't know him. We just met him at a bar. I swear.* But the man already knew this was a lie. And we knew that he knew.

A soft wind blew through the darkness. I began to wonder whether we'd already missed the last train. The glinty man took another kick at Hanada's face, but it wasn't a very enthusiastic one. Hanada dodged halfheartedly and the man's shoe whiffed pure air.

"Oh, you're gonna dodge now, are you?" the man said, giving Haneda a kick with his other leg. Then he nodded at the guy in the tracksuit and said, "You! Go take care of that other asshole."

The guy in the tracksuit bowed politely, walked over to Tanaka, and begin to punch. You could tell his heart wasn't in it, though. He had nothing against us, and we definitely weren't trying to start anything with him, so his punches didn't carry a lot of conviction. Tanaka managed to dodge them, for the most part. Meanwhile the guy in the brown jacket stood off to one side, hands in his pockets, gazing indifferently at the scene.

Yawn . . .

His whole demeanor said: *This ain't none of my business, but you two go right ahead and have your fun.*

At last the glinty man gave up on Hanada and headed toward me. His taut vitality sprung across the concrete and landed right in front of me. He was panting, breath peeling out in spirals.

"All right, Mr. Leather Jacket. Gimme your best shot."

That's right: on this particular evening I was wearing jeans and black boots with a black leather jacket. To be fair, I looked the part. At this comment, I realized that the glinty man was secretly intimidated by my leather jacket and boots.

"The fuck you waiting for?" he drawled. "Bring it on, mano a mano."

He spoke slowly, carefully. But this wasn't the deliberateness of a threat; it sounded more like he was trying to parse the surface tension of my black leather jacket. I was a stranger in black leather—a mystery man who had stood silently by, watching events unfold. All I had to do was stamp my foot and yelled "Boo!" and he probably would have flinched:

Flinch!

Of course all I actually did was look down at the ground and mutter something about how he had us all wrong, we didn't want to fight, we had no problem with him, please.

Mutter, mutter, mutter . . .

All of his hesitation immediately melted away. He spat out some line straight from a movie—"Shove it, pally"—and the next thing I knew, his fist was flying at my face.

Fwoosh!

I managed to move fast enough that he only hit my arm, which garnered the same quip he'd given Hanada: "Oh, you're gonna dodge now, are you?" Then he raised two fingers on his right hand and started jabbing at my eyes.

Stab!

I put my hands up in defense. "Ooh, you're putting up your dukes now, are you?" the man taunted. *Of course I am,* I thought. *These eyeballs aren't a couple of eggs I got at the supermarket.*

I must have done a good job of protecting my eyes, because the glinty man gave up and set about kicking my back instead. But he was losing steam by the minute, and it all seemed a little uninspired. How can I describe it? It was almost as if I was an old can of cola that he was trying to kick out from under a car . . . The echo of a distant train announcement wafted in on the wind, each syllable like a tiny bit of lint. That must be the last train. Or, if we're lucky, there may be one more.

Fwoosh . . .

The wind picked up again, tussling litter over the concrete:

Rustle, rustle, rustle . . .

Every so often, an automobile would Doppler by outside the fence:

Vrrruuuuuoooooooonnnn . . .

We were in that dark town at the back of the refrigerator, behind closed doors. Arms and legs clunked and thudded around the frigid landscape.

The boss in the brown jacket sauntered over our way. He had places to be. Noticing this, the glinty man became even more animated. Under his boss's gaze, he begin putting on a show, like an actor or a pro wrestler. He tried to act like he was playing a part in some epic struggle. Or perhaps the act of playing the part was itself the epic struggle.

"So anyways," said the guy in the brown suit. "It sounds like the real culprit was the drunk who ducked out at the station, and now you chumps are stuck paying his tab. To be frank, I feel sorry for you. Okay? So now that we're all on the same page, why don't we go get a drink and part ways like gentlemen?"

Thirty minutes later, the six of us were sitting together in a ramen shop. The last train had long since left, and this was the only place still open. The cook rattled around behind the counter, tidying up:

Rattle, clang, clatter . . .

Last call was closing in, and the men ordered beer as though their lives depended on it. *Have a beer,* they said. *Don't be shy,* they said. *Drink and be merry. Be merry. Be merry . . .* The man in the brown jacket kept talking about being merry. Which was fine for Tanaka and me, but not for poor Hanada, who sat over in the corner, staring at the floor, his face slowly rising like bread:

Bubble, bubble, bubble . . .

As a delegate for the Truth of the Matter, there was no way Hanada was going to be merry. But there was no point in trying to explain this, so Hanada just sat in his corner, holding the Truth of the Matter firmly in the back of his throat. He had swallowed it in order to keep it from coming back out, and now it was bubbling up through his face. Meanwhile, Tanaka and I tried our best to smile and say things like "Indeed!" and "Certainly!"

At some point, the glinty man looked over at me and asked:

"Hey, you some kinda professor?" His tone had changed completely. "I always had a lot of respect for teachers, you know. A teacher, huh? Drink up, drink up."

He poured more beer into my mug.

Glub, glub, glub . . .

After a few beers, the men had started asking questions like "What school you guys go to?" and "Whatcha studying?" in the course of which it came out that I was their teacher. The glinty man turned out to have so much respect for teachers that the guy in the brown suit started getting jealous, and took to trotting out his own resumé: expounding on the yakuza, the Business, the Organization, how the world was changing and they were making moves in the international scene.

Rattle, clang, clatter . . .

The sounds of closing time grew more pronounced.

Splash!

A bucket of mop water was tossed onto the curb. Time to close up shop. Our ordeal was over at last. We left the ramen shop slowly, desperate to hide our relief. The lights were out in all the stores at this hour, and no one hustled to catch any trains. The concrete gaped dark and vacant.

Gape . . .

Our footsteps echoed across the empty expanse:

Clop, clop, clop . . .

The glinty man, now several beers deep, was still writhing with vitality.

"Let's get another drink in Akasaka," he said. "I know this great joint . . ."

A chill went down my spine.

Shiver . . .

It was just a suggestion, but he was making it directly at me: "Come on, Teach! Let's go for another round!" Meanwhile the man in the brown jacket was striding off in the opposite direction. The glinty man raced off after him, then rushed back to yell: "Hey, assholes!"

Apparently he couldn't handle his alcohol, because he seemed pretty drunk after a handful of beers. We waited for what would follow "Hey, assholes," but the brown jacket was moving briskly, and the glinty man raced back down the dim street. He seemed desperate to be attached to somebody, anybody, there in the darkness. For our part, we wanted nothing more than to duck into an alleyway and put an end to the whole affair; but we also kind of felt that since we had come this far, we might as well see it through to the end. And so we shuffled along reluctantly after them. The glinty man's pale face would come racing out of the darkness and shout, "Hey, assholes!" before clattering back off into the gloom in hot pursuit of the brown jacket.

Clatter, clatter, clatter . . .

The city was completely empty. Nothing was out at this hour but the street, the sidewalk, the telephone poles, the boulevard trees, a plastic bucket, a pile of garbage bags, a payphone, a prostrate bicycle, aluminum shutters, darkened signs, black glass. The permafrost of the city stretched deep into the recesses of the refrigerator. From somewhere down in those depths, the glinty man raced back toward us.

Clatter, clatter, clatter . . .

He seemed frazzled.

"Hey, assholes!" he shouted. "Where'd you hide the boss man?"

Of course, we weren't hiding anybody anywhere, so the glinty man rushed off in a tizzy, back into the gloom.

Clatter, clatter, clatter . . .

Then he came careening back.

Clatter, clatter, clatter . . .

"You assholes put a hit on the boss!" he screamed. "You took him somewhere and knocked him off!"

This, of course, was news to us. We stood in the darkness with our mouths agape, speechless until the glinty man clattered away again:

Clatter, clatter, clatter . . .

Once again, we began shuffling down the street. In the distance, we could still hear his frantic footsteps racing this way and that. He must have lost track of the guy in the brown jacket. I guess he'd grown a little too attached to us.

Clatter, clatter, clatter . . .

Soon the patter of his feet began to assume an irregular, swerving rhythm, growing faster and more unhinged. We saw his face flash by at the far end of an alley.

Flash!

He was as full of vitality as ever.

Flash!

Then he was shooting through a different alley on the other side of the street.

Flash!

He was clearly terrified, all alone there in the darkness, desperately weaving his way through the grid of the entire neighborhood.

The three of us walked side-by-side, as slowly as we could go. We heard the glinty man approach from behind, but this time he avoided coming too close. There were three of us and only one of him, which only tripled the terror he felt, alone in the night. He gave us a wide berth, swerving and shouting as he flashed past: "You killed the boss, you fuckers!"

Then he scrambled away once more.

Clatter, clatter, clatter . . .

Like a kicked can of cola, the glinty man clattered off into the distance, disappearing into the night.

◉⊙◎

My back has turned into a refrigerator door. It's a thick rectangle, hard enough to knock on. It contains a large shelf that can hold up to four beers. And a yogurt. And ketchup and Worcestershire sauce and mayonnaise. There are eggs lined up along my shoulders. Everything is ice cold. My entire back feels frozen and heavy. My nose is running in the cold. A chill has fallen over the kitchen. My breath turns to steam and then disappears. My elbows are perched on my knees and my head rests in my hands. Then I hear Walnut's voice:

"Dad, I'm hooome!"

They're done jumping rope. Walnut's probably in the entryway, frantically trying to kick off her sneakers. I bet she's stepping on the heel of one shoe with the toe of the other. I hear the handles of the jump rope skittering down the hallway.

"It's cold in here!" she says. "Why don't you turn on the furnace?"

"Yeah, good idea. Do you know how?"

"Uh, yeah, it's just a switch. But I'm not allowed to turn it on unless there are adults in the house, right?"

"That's right."

Walnut drops her jump rope next to the desk and flips on the furnace. Our furnace has an ignition switch—no need for matches.

"Hey, Dad, what happened to the bomb?"

"The bomb? Oh—ha ha—it's in the fridge, safe and sound."

"You're not supposed to have bombs."

"I know. That's why I put it in the fridge."

"Psh. Stop acting like it's a real bomb."

"I mean, a bomb's a bomb."

"Is it going to blow up the refrigerator?"

"Not as long as it stays inside, nice and cold."

"Bombs don't explode when they're cold?"

"Of course not. A fuse can't light if it's frozen, right?"

"Oh, okay."

"Actually, that might not be true."

"Huh?"

"Hold on—you can totally start a fire on a cold morning. So I guess there's no reason you couldn't start a fuse in the fridge."

"You can light a match in the fridge?"

"Yeah. But what if the match was completely frozen, like a piece of ice? What would happen if you tried to strike it then?"

"Whoa, an ice match? That sounds pretty. But it also sounds

like it would shatter right away."

"An ice match—I like it. I bet an ice match would give off a chilly flame."

"Maybe it gives off snow!"

"Ha ha—a snow match! That's really nice. You strike it and it emits snow. Tiny little snowflakes cascading down from the tip."

"Ah—I want one! If we put a match in the fridge, do you think it will turn into a snow match?"

"Hmmmm . . ."

"Can I make one, Dad! I want to make a snow match!"

"Well, let's see . . ."

I gently peel my back off the refrigerator door and get to my feet. Next to the stove, I find a tiny box labeled PEACH BRAND SAFETY MATCHES. Returning to the fridge, I open the door. White air gapes before me.

"Should we just put them in here?" I ask.

"Yeah. Up there on the top shelf, next to the eggs. That's a good spot."

"Right here?"

"Yeah. The matches are mine, okay?"

"Of course, of course—I promise not to use them. Can I close the door now?"

Walnut glances at the bag of oysters.

"The bomb is asleep," she says.

"That's right." I shut the door. "It's sleeping."

The refrigerator's motor kicks in, humming itself cold.

"Hey, Dad? Who is it that sends these bombs again?"

"You're making it sound like terrorism."

"You're the one who called them bombs."

"Fair enough. They come from Mr. Mori. Remember him? You met him once a long, long time ago."

"Why does he keep sending them?"

"Well . . . Because . . ."

Ummm . . . uhhh . . . I start to hem and haw, unconsciously turning around to look at the refrigerator. A two-year-old version of Walnut sits inside, motionless.

"Well, a long time ago, Mr. Mori, he . . . uh . . . he fell asleep at the train station and, um, a robber came and . . . and this robber stole his favorite camera. So me and two friends went chasing after the robber, and we caught him and tied him up. And that's how we got Mr. Mori's camera back."

"Is that true?"

"Of course!"

"Then why do you sound like you're lying? You love telling lies."

"I swear! Mr. Mori had taken some important photos inside the camera."

"What kind of photos?"

"Well, they were the super valuable kind—more valuable than pictures of a UFO. I never got to see them, though."

"Really?"

"Yeah. But later Mr. Mori sent us some oysters to say thanks. And he sent them the next year, too. And ever since it's become kind of a habit for him. He's been doing it every year."

"That's a weird habit."

"Well, the thing about Mr. Mori is that he lost his memory."

"Huh?"

"This happened later, but one day a policeman came and conked him over the head, which gave him something called 'amnesia,' where you can't remember things that happened a long time ago. Since he can't remember the past, he just repeats the things he can remember like a habit."

I close the empty oyster box, pick up the polyurethane string, and carry all of it back to my room. I hold the box with both hands, which makes it feel like an urn. I look down at the name on the shipping label—MORI KAZUMA—and think: *it's like the name on a gravestone*. I immediately feel guilty for thinking this. What a mess.

"Hey Walnut! You've got a doctor's appointment—the ear, nose, and throat doctor."

"Again? Do I have to go?"

"It's your nose, missus. You want to get a bunch of bloody boogers again?"

"No . . ."

"Well I've got some shopping to do anyway. I'll walk you there."

"Fine . . ."

I grab a shopping bag, check my wallet, switch off the furnace, and lock all the windows. Walnut appears with her insurance card and a handkerchief.

"I need a dollar and thirty cents, Dad."

"Here you go—exact change."

The loose change clinks into Walnut's tiny palm. Her hand is so tiny I worry the coins will fall out.

"All right, let's go."

I close the front door behind us and double-check to make sure it's properly locked. Just when it seems like we're on our way, the faint jangle of the phone comes echoing out. Walnut and I look at each other. I've still got one hand on the doorknob.

"Hmm . . . What should I do?"

The door is locked—but who could it be? The Chairman? Hanada? Or even Mori himself? I think about the three of them, in that order, and when these thoughts have run their course, I'm left with the sensation of that endless silent phone call: the mute ear on the other end, a piece of butterscotch that grows until I'm enveloped in its amber. From somewhere between us comes the buzz of static, that little iron bug wriggling down the line and into my ear.

Buzz, crackle . . . Brrrrr, crack . . .

What should I do? The phone is ringing. My head is thinking about everything all at once, but my hand is frozen, fused to the door.

ABOUT THE AUTHOR

KATSUHIKO OTSUJI is the pen-name of avant-garde artist Genpei Akasegawa. Akasegawa was already a towering figure in the Japanese art world when he began writing fiction in the 1970s. In quick succession, he won the Chūō Kōron New Writers Award, the coveted Akutagawa Prize, and the Noma Prize for New Literature. Akasegawa continued writing as Otsuji throughout the 1980s, even as his artist-ego published best sellers and coined conceptual art terms like "Thomasson" and "Street Observations." Writing remained central to his practice even after he lost interest in fiction and abandoned the Otsuji moniker. In 1989, he won the Japanese Academy Award for Best Screenplay, for his biopic of Sen no Rikyū. In 1998, he wrote a best-selling book of essays, *The Senile Superpower (Rōjinryoku)*, which quickly became a cultural phenomenon.

ABOUT THE TRANSLATOR

MATTHEW FARGO has written and translated multiple books, including Akasegawa Genpei's *Hyperart: Thomasson* (Kaya Press, 2009). He lives in Tokyo.